MW01516073

Peril at the Point

Book 1 of
The Lamb's Bay Mysteries

By A. J. Fotheringham

Peril at the Point, Book 1 of The Lamb's Bay Mysteries,
is published by A. J. Fotheringham.
Copyright A. J. Fotheringham 2020
All rights reserved.
ISBN 9798637891818

With thanks to my editors and beta readers:
Marian Gallagher, Janet Klein and Joanne Giacomini
and to the members of the West Island Writers' Group
for their support and feedback.

Chapter 1

The sun rose out of the ocean and rode the horizon, sending pink and orange streamers across the pale dawn sky, driving back the gray clouds and gilding the sea birds that wheeled above the steel-colored waves. I was watching the sun's display as I drove so it was either a miracle or great reflexes that alerted me to the body lying across the road.

I swung the wheel hard, swerved off the road and braked. I let out a deep breath and turned off the car. It was July, the hottest month in these parts usually, so I had rolled down the windows on the Jeep to catch the breeze. But instead of me enjoying the cool dawn air, fear and adrenalin were making me sweat as if it were high noon. I passed a sleeve over my brow.

As I got out of the car, I could see a pair of sand-encrusted legs sticking out across the road at odd angles. I could hear the roar of the waves as they hit the nearby rocks that signaled the beginning of the rocky outcrop into the ocean known as Paxton's Point. The birds were circling, calling to each other. The girl and I were silent.

As I approached the body, I saw it was that of a young woman. I was about to kneel down and check for a pulse when suddenly, I heard an engine cough. I scanned for its source. From further down the line of sandy hillocks, a dune buggy shot out across the road and onto the flat wet beach and ran south, silhouetted against the burning sun. Someone was in a hurry but it wasn't the girl and it wasn't me. I bent back to my task. No pulse. I stood up. My breakfast appointment with my friend Brody Paxton would have to wait.

Some start to the day I thought as I picked up my cell and called 911. After I'd connected with the police, and told them about my discovery, I hung up and shook my head. Heck, I shouldn't be so upset about the bad start to the day. After all, that woman had a worst start – or end— than I did.

I sat in my car and waited for the police. I knew I should have been paying more attention. Driving the shore road took concentration. It skirted the dunes and scrubland that bordered the beach and a strong wind overnight could create mini dunes in unprotected areas or dump the detritus of the sea on the pockmarked asphalt. You had to be alert and ready to swerve. You shouldn't be looking at the sky, but I was.

Dawn was particularly spectacular at this time of the year and I've always been a fan of the show the sun would put on when it rose each day. Only this morning, the sun was angry and I thought of the old saying, "red sky at morning, sailors warning." What had started out as a simple drive to a friend's house was now a criminal matter About 15 minutes later, the quiet beachfront had been invaded by a couple of police officers, an ambulance and a couple of EMTs. A few early morning joggers were being questioned as I had been. I had nothing to tell them.

I didn't recognize the girl and I'd had a good look at her while I waited for the police chief to show up. Blonde, twenty something, I guessed. She was wearing cutoff jeans and a torn T-shirt. One sneaker lay beside her naked feet. There was no sign of the other. The odd thing was that we were a good 40 feet from the pounding surf and the girl's hair and clothing were wet and plastered to her body. It's tough to drown on the shore road. Someone must have moved her.

I told Lester Spriggs, the police chief, about the dune buggy. He'd taken note of it but I doubted he'd find it. Dune buggies were pretty common around here and, because of the sun, I'd been unable to get a clear look at it. All I knew was the driver appeared to have short hair, but I couldn't guess at the rest.

Lester told me to stay put for the time being and I watched his lanky six-foot frame amble back to the police cruiser. I saw him talking on the radio, probably to his dispatcher, maybe about the dune buggy. Lester was an old friend from grade school. He looked laid back and calm, but the set of his jaw told me he was concerned.

Our town, Lamb's Bay, was a quiet community. A dead woman lying in the middle of the road was a complication the local police rarely had to deal with. But they had been bier latterly, especially since Brody's wife, Gina, had been found dead on the nearby rocks only four days ago and his 12-year-old daughter, Ruby, had disappeared.

The police's first assumption had been that Gina had fallen from the cliff side of the point and drowned, but none of us believed that. The police were now treating it as a possible homicide and kidnapping, but so far there had been little headway in the case. And no trace of Ruby.

I figured Lester was worried that the two deaths were linked. But the woman was a stranger, of that I was sure, and couldn't have any link to Gina and Ruby. Or could she?

As I wondered about the girl, who she was and how she had ended up here, Brody Paxton turned up. He'd seen my car and the cruisers from his house on the point he said. He'd been worried when I hadn't turned up and had begun scanning the shore with his telescope. When he saw the flashing lights, he'd known there was trouble. Too bad he had not been using his telescope earlier. He might have seen the person who dumped the woman on the road. Lester asked Brody if he'd seen anything but he hadn't.

Brody was drawn and looked exhausted. He'd sounded tense when he had called me earlier, asking me to come over right away.

"Did you ask Lester if there was any news about . . .?" I let my voice trail off.

"No news," Brody said. "That's why I called you. I want to talk to you about something."

Just then, Lester walked over to where we were standing.

"Hilly, you can go," Lester said to me. "Just drop by my office and give a statement later today. We're going to move her now."

I nodded, but I didn't move. Brody and I stood by the Jeep and waited until the woman had been loaded into the ambulance and begun her journey to the morgue. Somehow I knew I had to see her on her way. Because if I didn't see the road clear once more, I knew that in my dreams, I'd forever find her turning up in front of my car and my fear would be that one night I wouldn't swerve in time. I didn't need nightmares like that.

"Going back to town?" Lester asked as he drove level with the Jeep and braked.

"No, like I said, I was on my way to see Brody. I'll see you later."

He nodded. "Well, you think and see if you remember anything else, Hilly, and don't forget to come by and make that statement." He drove off, his wheels creating a fine mist of sand that hung in the humid morning air for just a moment, then was blown away on the breeze.

"Doesn't sound like you're under suspicion," Brody said calmly.

"No, I'm not," I replied. "Besides, in the three years since I moved back home, I haven't had as much as a parking ticket. I'm clean and Lester knows it."

"Then why are you standing there holding onto your driver's license and registration? Put them away and let's go," Brody said. "I've got cinnamon buns waiting. And I need to discuss something with you." He headed for his car. A minute later he was headed back to Paxton Point.

I glanced down at the license I still held in my hand. I read my full name. Hilaria Barton-Cheswick. I winced. My father, who'd taught Latin and English at a nearby college, had been fascinated by the Greek and Roman myths. I guess he never realized that calling me Hilaria had made me a target at school. The joke got old fast and the other kids soon got used to calling me Hilly, a nickname that stayed with me to this day.

I only used my initials on the business cards for my research company. However, the law required my full name be on my license and, when the first officer on the scene asked for my ID, I could see the corners of his mouth twitching. Lucky thing the police chief and I had gone to school together and he knew I was not a murderer.

I stowed the license in my purse, then backed the Jeep onto the road and drove until I took the turnoff for the point.

Paxton Point was a rocky anomaly, a lumpy growth on the smooth sandy skin that stretched along the coast from Port MacKenzie south 80 miles to Roxton. The point stuck out into the sea for almost a mile and was about half a mile across at its widest. At its tip rose a lighthouse that had been tended by the Paxton's for several generations before automation had occurred in the late 1930s. The last of the Paxtons, Brody, still lived out on the point, though he managed and owned several rental cottages on the beachfront closer to town.

His wife, Gina Hunt, had been my best friend. We'd been close and she had stood by in the tough times left my sister Vesta and me with my father.

I never did understand what Gina saw in Brody. He was five years older than us, short and wiry, a quiet man with set ways who was known for his honesty and loyalty. Gina married him as soon as she turned 18. I'd been the maid of honor. We'd not seen much of each other in the early years of their marriage. I went off to college and then worked in the city. When my relationship with my former partner had imploded and my father got ill, I'd come back to Lamb's Bay. I'd looked after my dad and set up my Internet-based business here. Brody and Gina and I had taken up again as if the years had barely gone by.

I parked outside the Paxton's cottage. As always, when I stepped out of the car, I couldn't resist taking a deep breath of the sea air. Out on the point, the air seemed somehow wetter, fraught with the urgency of the waves. You could smell the salt as well as the rotting seaweed. Somehow it spoke to me of our childhood and the adventures we had.

The early morning fog had burned off, but there were still a few bits of it floating around. The angry sun was infusing them with tints of gold and burnt orange. I turned away from the sea view and looked back towards the beach road. A low remnant of fog drifted across the road for a moment, then whirled back towards the beach. For just that moment it had shown up the sharp contrasts between the rocky, grass-tufted point and the sandy shore, giving the impression that we had passed across an unseen bridge into another world, a rocky island where anything might happen.

Brody appeared and cleared his throat.

"Sorry," I said. "The view always gets to me."

"Know what you mean," he said. "I've lived with it all my life and yet every day it seems new and fresh, the mood changes with the light." He stopped and scanned the shoreline for a moment, then dropped his eyes to mine. "Come on in, coffee and buns in the kitchen."

I stuffed my car keys in my jeans pocket and followed him inside and down the hall to the kitchen with its view right out onto the ocean. I sat at the table in the bay window and looked out. The sun had had moved higher up the sky and the light in the kitchen was bright and full of promise. But I had been there when storms were threatening over the sea. You could watch them rolling towards the land and Brody was right. The mood of the view changed dramatically, especially at those times. I shuddered. Somehow my snug house located on Dune Road, about a mile from the beach suddenly seemed like an oasis of safety and calm.

A cup of coffee and a cinnamon bun had materialized in front of me. The smell of the cinnamon and the view of the creamy icing sliding across the bun onto the plate were irresistible. For next few minutes, Brody and I indulged ourselves with the sweet buns and the dark rich coffee he'd made.

Brody took a second bun. I didn't know how he could take an extra sugar load like that. I could feel the icing coursing through my blood stream already and knew I'd have to run an extra mile or two today to work it off.

While Brody ate, I looked around. I noticed Gina's things had been left just as if she had stepped out for a moment. Across the hall I could see her knitting bag still sitting by her rocking chair, patiently waiting for her to come back and turn out scarves and sweaters for Brody and all her friends. But Gina wasn't coming back.

The day Gina died and Ruby disappeared, Brody had spent a whole day working at one of the beach houses he owned. He and Shad Benson had reshingled the roof. Gina had been at home with their daughter Ruby. When he drove home in the twilight of a beautiful summer evening, he'd seen more than the dying sun lighting up the sky. There'd been the flashing lights of police cruisers. Two people out kayaking had seen the body on the rocks under the point and called 911. Ruby was missing. There were still no leads, no clues.

"Aren't you wondering why I called you?" Brody finally asked.

"Well of course." The incident on the beach road had driven his urgent call at 5 a.m. today out of my mind. I recalled I had been dozing fitfully when the phone rang. "Hilly I have to talk to you. Come now. Or soon."

"Brody? It's 5 a.m. Can't it wait till I've showered and had breakfast?"

"Hilly it's important. Shower if you want but I'll supply breakfast. I need to talk to you." And the phone had gone dead.

Brody cleared his throat and I was back in the cottage eating cinnamon buns and drinking coffee. I looked across the table at Brody. "So what's up," I asked.

"Gina was murdered,"

"Yeah, Brody," I said. "We know."

"No, but I think she was killed because she saw something or someone. And that may be why Ruby ran away."

"Brody? What could Gina have seen that would make someone kill her? And Ruby …" I paused. How did you tell a father that every police officer you knew was convinced Ruby was dead too, or worse, kidnapped by a crazy person who was doing who knew what to her? I reached across the table and touched his hand. He looked up at me.

"You think I'm crazy. You think like everyone else that Ruby is dead, don't you."

I didn't know what to answer. "Brody," I started to say, "I, I …"

He got up and paced the room. He passed a hand across the back of his neck, then stopped and stood facing out the window towards the sea that was now sparkling in the mid-morning light.

"I couldn't sleep last night, so I made some coffee and started to go through Gina's things in case there was some clue the cops missed. I started with her bedside table and dresser." He stopped for a minute and I could sense the sob that he was trying so hard to control. "I found this."

He crossed to the kitchen counter and picked up a file folder. He came over and sat back down across the table from me. "I think Gina's death and Ruby's disappearance have something to do with this stuff in the folder." He was holding it clutched to his chest.

"You knew Gina all her life, Hilly, I have to ask you. Did she ever mention a treasure to you?"

"A treasure?" I smiled. "I think you and Ruby were her treasures, Brody. She loved you both so dearly."

Brody nodded. "Yes she did. But I said treasure not treasures. Did she ever mention a treasure or someone looking for a treasure?"

I shook my head. "No. Sounds like something out of a kid's story." I frowned. Had Gina taken up writing mystery stories or something?

"Brody, stop being cryptic. Just tell me what you think all this is about. And what treasure are you talking about?"

"So Gina never told you about the treasure of Paxton Point?" Brody placed the file folder on the table and laid both hands on top of it. "It's one of the local tales – every few years some local historical nut does a write-up about it in the paper. The belief was that some men who robbed a bank had buried or hidden the gold bars they stole out her on the point. They never came back for them."

"The treasure of Paxton Point? No I don't think I've ever run into that local tale. But what kind of a treasure could Paxton Point have? It's solid rock."

Brody smiled. "That's where you are wrong. Don't you remember? There are some caves on the sea side of the point itself, though not all are accessible anymore. Remember that landslide about 8 years ago? Now a couple of them are only accessible to divers. There are some that you can get into from the beach at low tide, but they flood as soon as the tide turns. There are also chimneys in the rocks that lead up from the caves to the top of the point. We explored them when we were teenagers. Who knows whether those bank robbers used one of those places to hide the gold? Though to date, no one has ever found it."

I nodded. I remember now. I hadn't thought about the caves in years. "You think there's a treasure down there? Brody, I ..."

Brody held up one hand. "Let me finish. The story goes like this . . ."

Chapter 2

August 1933

Chrissie Paxton was watching her husband Myron head for the lighthouse when she heard a car engine. She turned in time to see a beat-up black sedan rolling down the point road towards the cottage. She turned back towards Myron and noticed he had stopped and was watching the car's progress.

It was getting towards sundown, the wind was picking up and Myron needed to be up tending to the light, not taking care of visitors.

When he started back towards her, Chrissie waved him off. She could handle another couple of summer tourists wanting to take photos. Not that they'd get much of a picture at this time of the day despite the blood red sun which was streaking the sky with orange and gray streamers as it began its nightly descent behind the dunes bordering the sea.

Myron stopped, shrugged then turned his back on the car and kept walking towards the lighthouse. Chrissie noticed he was walking faster now. It was a long climb up to check on the light and the sun was sinking fast.

The car crunched on the shingle drive in front of the cottage and came to a stop beside the Paxton's truck. Chrissie watched as two men slowly climbed out of the sedan and stood uncertainly in the dying rays of the evening sun. The early evening wind off the ocean had a touch of autumn in it today and Chrissie shivered in her thin cotton summer dress. She felt chilled head to toe and a sense of dread began to build inside her as the two men advanced towards her.

Chrissie shrugged the feeling off. She was two steps from the front door and the shotgun Myron kept handy beside it. She knew how to use it too. He'd taught her well. She took two steps back and leaned against the doorjamb, her right hand reaching out and finding the comforting coolness of the shotgun's barrel.

"Evening," she said. "There's no lighthouse visits after sundown. Sorry."

"Aunt Chrissie," one of the men said. "You don't remember me?"

Chrissie squinted. The sun's display was making it hard to see clearly, but she did detect something familiar about the man. What was it?

"It's me, Elmont, Elmont Thacker."

"Elmont? Rita's boy?" Chrissie let go of the shotgun and shaded her eyes. Yes there was that wild blonde hair and those bright blue eyes. She smiled, remembering. "Why Elmont, it's been… well a long time. Is your mama in town too?" Chrissie had not seen her cousin Rita for three years since she remarried and moved to Texas. Elmont had been 16 then and had gone with them, hell bent on becoming a cowboy he'd said.

"Aunt Chrissie, of course it's me."

The young man stepped closer and Chrissie could see him clearer now. The young boy look was still there, but there was a look that comes with maturity and hardship too, a look she'd seen on many a man's face as the country had crawled its way through the early 1930s.

"Mama's not here though," he said, fiddling with the hat he held in his hands. "She's in California."

"California? What happened to Texas?" Chrissie asked, taking a couple of steps closer to the men. "Is she okay?" Rita had been her best friend as well as her cousin when they were growing up.

Elmont smiled. "She's fine. Things didn't go too smooth with Ed so they split. She got married last month to a man who works in the movie business out in Hollywood. Yup, she's fine." He cleared his throat. "Um this here's Dan, my friend. We're passing through and thought we'd say hello and …"

"Hello?" Chrissie suddenly remembered her manners. The sense of dread had passed. Must have been my imagination. She extended a hand to Elmont and then pulled him into a quick hug. "Why you can say more than hello to your aunty who looked after you when you were a boy. Come on in. Have you eaten?"

Elmont smiled shyly. "No, Aunty Chrissie. Me and Dan was gonna find a hotel for the night and get a meal along the coast before heading off … heading towards where we is going."

"Where are you going," Chrissie asked, ushering the two men into the house.

"Got a line on some jobs up to Port MacKenzie," Elmont said. "So we're heading there."

"Guess being a cowboy didn't pan out, huh?"

"No ma'am. Seems horses and I don't get along," Elmont said. Chrissie noticed Elmont was doing all the talking. Dan was silent, but his eyes were everywhere, scanning her kitchen as if looking for something special. Chrissie frowned; the man looked creepy. Then she shook off her suspicions. After all, Elmont had always been a good boy so why should she doubt his friend? Maybe he was just the silent, shy type, she thought.

While the two men washed up, Chrissie split up the remainder of the stew she had served for supper and laid the plates on the table. She still had that odd sense of something being not quite right, but family is family. She took a deep breath and smiled at the two men as they dug into their stew.

"You boys can stay here tonight if you like," she said. "Cheaper than the hotels – it's season right now and the rates are kind of high. There's the boys' bedroom you can use."

"Thanks," Dan said. His voice was deep and somehow hollow. It made Chrissie start when he spoke. He lifted his eyes from his plate and looked right at her and, for a moment, she had a glimpse of a black nothingness that seemed to hover behind his eyes. Then he blinked and it was gone. "You sure your boys won't mind? Elmont here said you got two boys, right?"

"Yeah," Chrissie said. "But they're both working down to Roxton for the summer at the mill, and staying with Cousin Brian and his family. You remember Brian," she said forcing herself not to look at Dan but at Elmont, familiar Elmont, the little boy she had cuddled and looked after when he was small.

Elmont smiled. "Oh yeah," he said. "I remember him. So they won't be back tonight?"

"No," Chrissie said as she poured the men large cups of coffee to go with the rest of her apple pie. "No they won't be here. Too bad, they would have liked to see you again."

"Yeah, that's too bad," Dan intoned. Then his serious mouth lifted its corners and he added "but now we got somewhere to sleep so I guess it isn't all that bad is it?"

Chrissie somehow wasn't that sure. She was getting that sense of dread again, a feeling that things weren't as they seemed. But surely they must be okay, her nephew and his friend just passing through. Living out on the point alone with Myron was making her suspicious she decided. They should have company more often. It was lonely with the boys away.

After supper, Elmont and his friend went outside for a smoke, leaving Chrissie with the dishes. As she soaped and rinsed the plates and cups, she washed away her feelings of anxiety. It was the times, she thought. The thirties had been tough on everyone. Men out of work roamed the countryside, some looking for honest work, others for an easy dollar. After Myron and she had come home from the market in time to catch one ruffian stealing things from their cottage, Myron had taught her how to use the shotgun. She wasn't a great shot, but she could at least hit a target, though not right in the centre. When Dan and Elmont came back inside, Chrissie was in her chair working on some knitting and listening to the radio. Her favorite radio serial was on, The Spensers, the weekly adventures of a family who ran a filling station and garage. Elmont and Dan sat quietly listening until the program ended. Chrissie turned the radio off and stood up.

"Well, I'm going to turn in," she said. "You fellas need anything? I put blankets and sheets on the beds. And there's a towel each for the morning."

"Nah, Aunty Chrissie," Elmont said. "That'll be fine. Say, what time does Uncle Myron come down from the lighthouse station?"

"Myron? Not long after dawn. He puts out the light and then cleans and polishes it so he's all ready for the evening. Then he comes down for breakfast," She smiled. "He'll be real happy to see you again, Elmont. Well, good-night." She pecked Elmont on the cheek and nodded at Dan. "Sleep well."

"Night," said Elmont. Dan stayed silent.

Alone in her room Chrissie changed into her nightgown, said her prayers, then climbed into bed and put out the light. The moon was riding high and shining through the lacy curtains on the window. She loved nights when the moon lit up the room. It was like a friend telling her it was watching over her while she slept alone at night. Alone while Myron tended his light, sending its warning about the rocky shoals to all nearby shipping and monitoring the short-wave radio for any emergency calls.

"Marry a lighthouse keeper, you'll sleep alone," her mother had warned her. But Myron was her choice and as she settled down to sleep, she reflected that it had been a happy one, even though she had to sleep alone a lot of the time. As she drifted off, she wondered again about Elmont's strange friend and what her cousin Rita was doing in California. In Hollywood, no less. Who'd have thought she would end up there?

When Chrissie woke hours later, the early rays of sunlight were inching their way across her quilt. She glanced at the clock and realized she was running behind. She should have been up by now making Myron breakfast. Then she remembered her visitors from the night before. "Goodness, they said they wanted an early start. Got to feed them before they leave," she said out loud as she threw on a housedress and raked a comb through her hair.

Pulling a cardigan around her shoulders to ward off the early morning chill, Chrissie reached for the doorknob, turned it and opened the door.

It was quiet in the house, almost too quiet.

"Those boys must be real tired if they're still sleeping," she mumbled as she put the water on to boil for coffee. Flapjacks. That would fill them up well for the day ahead and besides, they were Myron's favorites. Myron. Where was he? He should have been down from the light by now? Chrissie frowned and looked out the window. The truck and boys' car were still parked outside. Perhaps she'd better go check to see if everything was okay.

Chrissie headed for the front door and was just reaching for the handle when the door opened and Dan came in. His hair was tousled and he looked as if he had slept in his clothes.

"Going somewhere, Miss Chrissie?" Dan asked. His tone was harsh and Chrissie started at it.

"I was just going to see why Myron wasn't down from the light yet," she said, pulling her cardigan closer about her shoulders. "He should have been down by now. You boys been out walking? Where's Elmont?"

Dan cleared his throat, then he smiled. "Yeah, we been walking. Went to see what the beach looks like at low tide."

He took Chrissie by the elbow and steered her back to the kitchen. "Elmont's up to the light talking to his Uncle Myron," he said. "They'll be along shortly, Myron said he's got to fix something, I didn't quite understand what, but they're coming, don't you worry. Coffee ready?"

Chrissie didn't like being pushed back towards the kitchen by Dan. She pulled her arm free and stood by the stove looking at this stranger. She hadn't liked him from the start and he was giving her that creepy feeling again. Dan stared back at her with those bottomless eyes and that annoying smile.

"Yeah coffee's ready. You want some?" She moved the coffee pot onto the warming section of the stove, then looked back at Dan expectantly.

He shook his head. "Not right now. I'm gonna put our gear into the car and go get some gas down at the village. Elmont gave me directions. He wants to visit some more with you and his uncle. I'll be back shortly."

Chrissie stared at Dan's back as he left the room. She could hear him walking down the hall to her boys' bedroom. For some reason, she didn't want to move. She felt transfixed, as if Dan had to go before she could act or think or feel again. Chrissie felt chilled to the bone as she stood by the hot stove waiting for that man to leave her house. A couple of minutes later he passed by the kitchen door, a pair of duffle bags over his shoulder. "See ya later," he said. And then he was gone.

Chrissie heard the door open and slam shut. Footsteps crunched on the path outside the open window. She heard the car start up and turned in time to see it pass the window and head down the point to the shore road. As if in a trance, she watched it go until it was a black dot against the endless golden dunes.

She shivered again. She half hoped he wouldn't come back, but she knew Elmont would be waiting for him so they could travel to Port Mackenzie and their jobs. Jobs were important these days. No one took them lightly. And Elmont was lucky to have one waiting for him.

Flapjacks. Yessir. She'd make her very best ones with a side of bacon and while that creepy Dan was gone, she and Myron and Elmont could have a nice family visit. She smiled to think of Elmont and Myron up in the light. Elmont had always been fascinated by the lighthouse. Whenever he and his mother had been out on the point, he'd pestered Myron until he let him and the boys run up its winding stairs all the way to the top and the amazing view of the shoreline and the sea.

Chrissie busied herself making a pile of flapjacks, enough for six hungry men, not just three. She fried up the extra bacon she'd been saving and set the table with her best china. She hummed to herself as she worked. It sure was nice to have Elmont visiting her. She wondered how Rita was doing with husband number three. She shook her head. Times had changed. When they were girls, why a woman stayed with her man. Now, women and men divorced it seemed all the time.

Her food was ready and the men still hadn't made an appearance. Chrissie began to fret. That damn creepy Dan would be back shortly and…

Chrissie decided it was time for action. Myron and Elmont were probably chewing the fat up there at the light and forgot the time. She'd just have to go get them. She paused as she reached the front door to pull off her apron and smooth her dress. As she did, her glance lit on the space beside the door, the space where her shotgun was kept. It wasn't there.

Chrissie froze in place. The shotgun. It was there last night when Elmont and Dan arrived. And Myron hadn't been down from the light yet and…

A wave of anger swept through Chrissie. Somehow she just knew Dan had taken the shotgun. Of all the nerve. That creep… And then the anger was replaced by fear, fear that not only had Dan taken the shotgun but that… <u>Dear God. No. Myron</u>.

Chrissie threw the door open and ran as fast as she could up the path to the lighthouse. Her feet kicked up stones as she ran and the chill morning wind tore at her hair and dress. "Myron," she called. "Myron."

She knew there was trouble before she reached the keeper's station. She could feel it. She wrenched the door open and called as she entered the small building. But there was no response and no sign anyone was there. The light. Dan mentioned the lighthouse. She swung out the door across to the lighthouse itself towering above her. She gripped the door handle, yanking it open and ran into the cool dark interior of the lighthouse. The base area was a round room with shelves for storage. Supplies lined the walls and were piled on the floor as well. But Chrissie, squinting in the gloom saw there was something else lying on the floor.

"Myron," she screamed. She flew to his side and crouched down beside him. He was tied up and gagged. His eyes were closed and she felt herself choking with fear and terror. Myron, her Myron. Her love, her husband. Was he, was he…

She reached out and touched his forehead, his closed eyes. She smoothed his hair and suddenly, the eyes snapped open, Myron's eyes, blue as the sky above the sea.

"Myron, oh Myron." Her tears spilled down her cheeks and onto his face as she wrestled with the gag. She finally managed to undo the knot and flung the gag away from her.

"Chrissie," Myron said. "Are you okay? Did that bastard touch you?"

"Myron, Myron," Chrissie bent and kissed his lips. "I'm fine. Who did this to you? Was it that Dan fellow? I didn't trust him the moment I met him, I… "

".It was Rita's bastard son, Elmont. Who's Dan?" Myron asked, struggling to a sitting position. "Help me with these damn ropes. I get my hand on that fellow, he'll rue the day he ever showed his face around here again."

"Elmont? Elmont did this to you? I can't believe that," Chrissie said as she tugged and pulled at the knots binding Myron's hands. Suddenly they gave way and she sat back on her heels as Myron undid the ropes around his ankles.

"Yes, it was Elmont," Myron said. "I was just coming out of the station, when there he was. 'Remember me, Uncle Myron,' the little bastard says. 'It's me, Elmont, Rita's boy.' So I says 'hello' and he says, 'Come on Uncle Myron, let me climb the light and see the view, like we did when I was a kid.' I was tired, wanted my coffee, said we could go up later and then I turned away to walk to the house." Myron rubbed his ankles. "That's when the little bastard hit me. Don't remember nothing else till you woke me up." He reached out and grabbed Chrissie holding her closely to him. "Are you okay? What the hell happened?"

"Elmont and his friend Dan turned up, that was the car arriving as you were going to the light," Chrissie said. "I gave them supper and let them stay the night. Elmont seemed fine." She looked up at Myron. "You sure he was the one hit you? Not that creepy friend of his, Dan?"

"Dan who?" Myron asked. "I never saw anyone but Elmont." Myron let go of Chrissie and started to his feet. He pulled her up beside him. "Are they still here? What are they doing?"

"Well," Chrissie said, "that Dan, he's gone for a while. Went to gas up the car because they are supposed to drive to Port Mackenzie for some jobs today. But I haven't seen Elmont since last night and … oh Myron."

"What?" Myron asked as he reached for the door handle.

"The shotgun."

"What about the shotgun?" Myron asked, grabbing her by the shoulders and shaking her. "Chrissie, what about the shotgun?"

She pulled away. "It's missing. It was by the door last night. It wasn't there this morning."

"You had two strangers stay the night in the house and you didn't take the shotgun to the bedroom with you?" Myron stared down at her.

Chrissie's tears started to fall again. "Dan was the stranger. Elmont was family. I didn't think…"

"Come on," Myron said. "We've got to find out what's going on. How long has that Dan fellow been gone?"

"Well, I made some flapjacks and bacon and …"

"What?"

"I wanted to make everyone a nice breakfast, so about half an hour, I guess."

"And Elmont?"

"Told you. I haven't seen him. He's probably out walking the beach or having a smoke or something."

Myron peered cautiously out of the lighthouse door. Chrissie stood close behind him. "See anything?" she asked.

"Seems clear," he said. "Come on. We'll get to the truck and drive straight to the police chief's office."

"But Myron, what about Elmont?"

"Chrissie, wake up. Elmont hit me. Dan stole the shotgun. Something's not right."

Myron grabbed Chrissie's hand and they ran to the truck and quickly climbed in. They always kept the keys in the ignition, but there were no keys hanging there now.

"Damn," Myron said. "Bastards must have taken them. Come on."

"Where we going?" Chrissie asked as she climbed out of the truck.

"We'll take the rowboat and head over towards the Granger's dock down the beach. They've got a telephone. Come on."

Chrissie and Myron scrambled down the rocky path to where they kept their rowboat. At low tide it was barely afloat, but the tide had been coming in for the past hour and the rowboat rode at its mooring jauntily as the two reached the small jetty.

Myron let go of Chrissie hand. "I'll get the oars, you climb in," he said.

Chrissie ran over to the rowboat's line and pulled the craft close beside the jetty. Just as she was about to climb in, she looked down to ensure her footing would be secure. That's when she saw the blood sloshing about in water at the bottom of the boat, the blood that also soaked the front of Elmont's white shirt. He lay there with his throat slit from ear to ear, his blonde hair gleaming in the morning sun.

Chrissie screamed. She screamed louder than the circling gulls. As a wave of nausea and revulsion hit her, she crumpled to the jetty.

Chapter 3

I stared at Brody over the rim of my coffee cup. He'd gone silent on me. He'd told me a tale of a treachery and murder but hadn't uttered one word about missing gold.

"Uh Brody," I asked, "It that the whole story? I mean… "

Brody held up a hand. "Hold your horses. I'm not finished."

"Okay," I said. "I'm waiting. But will the words "missing gold bars" be used anytime soon?" The sugar rush from the cinnamon buns had faded and the effects of my dramatic find on the beach, plus the early start to the day, were taking their toll. Despite three coffees, I was beginning to feel the need to lie down and take a nap. "Brody," I prompted. "The gold?"

"Ah yes," Brody said. "Well, it turned out that Elmont and Dan were on the run."

"I figured that one out. Go on."

"There had been an armoured car robbery – a gang of six men got away with cash and some gold bars. The feds tracked them to a farmhouse not far from Lamb's Bay, but by the time they raided the place, all they found were four bodies and most of the cash and some of the gold. Ten gold bars were missing. Along with Elmont and Dan."

"So the "treasure" is gold bars from the 1930s?"

"Yup," Brody said. "Never did find it. Dan got captured by the feds a couple of days after he left Paxton Point and wouldn't tell where the loot was hidden. He went to jail, escaped twice. The first time, he was recaptured about five miles from here. That's why everyone figured he must have hidden the gold around here and was coming back for it. The second time he escaped, he tried to hold up a bank for a little spending money and ended up getting gunned down. He hung on in hospital for a week, but never spoke, never gave up his hiding place."

I nodded. "But everyone thought he buried it somewhere on the point with Elmont, that maybe Elmont showed him some great hiding place and then Dan killed him."

"The feds searched a lot of the point and the caves and even this house," Brody said. "But there wasn't any sign of the gold."

"Do you think it's here?" I asked.

Brody shook his head. "If no one found it yet, Dan probably hid it somewhere else in the area. But every now and then, the Paxtons have had to chase off yet another bunch of treasure hunters. So, Hilly, what do you think?"

"That's quite a yarn," I said, suppressing a yawn. "So you think someone got Gina interested in this stuff and that's why she was killed? I don't know, Brody."

"Look, Hilly," Brody said. "It's the only thing that has turned up since, since, since she's been gone. There has to be some reason she researched this old story." He thrust the folder at me. "Do me a favor, Hilly. Take a look at this stuff. Check your resources and see if anyone is expressing an interest in all this. It could mean something, perhaps help the cops find her killer and Ruby's kidnapper." His eyes pleaded with me and I found myself taking the proffered folder.

"It's really the police's job," I said. "Brody, you should let them do their work."

"Police." Brody spat the word out. "Been six days tomorrow and nothing, no clues and no sign of Ruby. She could be …" His voice faltered and tears welled up in his eyes. The Brody Paxton I knew was not prone to tears. But he was a husband who had lost his wife and a father whose daughter was missing. The tough exterior he always cultivated was breaking down. I swallowed and looked away. It was hard to say no and in the end, I knew I couldn't. "I'll do my best, Brody," I said. "But I can't promise …"

Brody gave me in a quick hug and then, embarrassed, stepped back. "Sorry, Hilly, I'm, well, just do what you can. I can pay you know."

"Pay? Brody, we are talking about Gina and Ruby here. Forget that word." I turned to go, then looked back. "Brody, you should get some help. It's not good here, alone on this rock. Have you asked for some counseling?"

Brody waved me away. "Go home, Hilly. Counseling isn't for the likes of me. I'll be fine. Just let me know if you find anything out. God bless." He ushered me out the door and closed it behind me a little faster than usual. I could sense his need to be alone with the pain, so I headed for my Jeep, climbed in and drove down the point to the shore road.

I rode home from Brody's with my head in a whirl. His story about the armoured car robbers and the murder of Elmont was disturbing. It was even more disturbing that it could be linked to Gina's disappearance. Why had she been researching that old story? Something must have set her off. It upset me that she had undertaken the research on her own—I was her best friend—or so I thought. I was used to doing research, it was my job after all, and I would have been happy to help her out if looking up historical information from the 30s had become one of her interests. So why the secrecy? Why had she gone out on her own?

I chewed on this thought most of the way home. I drove carefully, half expecting another body to turn up in the middle of the road, though the odds on two turning up in the same day were not good. By the time I pulled into my driveway, I was no further ahead in my thoughts about Gina. I picked up my mail and was sorting through it as I stepped into the cool front hall. One envelope caught my eye. It was a brown manila one addressed in block letters. I was about to open it when the phone started ringing.

I dashed down the hall into my office and scooped up the receiver. "Barton Cheswick," I said. When thinking up a name for my company, my two last names had naturally provided the answer. They sounded solid, like a law firm. The name had been well received so it stayed. Clients preferred doing business with a firm that sounded blue chip instead of "Hilly's Research."

"Hilly? Hi."

I stood still, the sound of that greeting echoing in my ear.

"Hilly, are you there? Answer please, it's important."

I was flashing back to three years before, to a time when that voice had been such an integral part of my life, to a time when I was the Barton half of Mayfair and Barton, Security and Investigations.

"Hilly?" The voice sounded frail, far away as if coming from my past. But the clock striking ten in the hallway brought me down to earth. This was now, not then, and Zachary Mayfair was on the other end of my phone.

I took a deep breath and spoke. "Zach?"

"Hilly," the voice said and I could hear the relief in the way he spoke my name. "I, I'm glad I caught you. We, um, need to talk about, about some stuff."

"Talk?" I said. "I think we were all talked out three years ago. I mean, what, what do you want Zach?" My surprise was slowly fading and I was feeling anger again. Anger at all those years I wasted living with him, making him the centre of my life when he spent his spare time chasing other women. Some investigator I had turned out to be. Couldn't even figure out that my boyfriend was not only cheating on me, but with half of the women I had stupidly considered my friends. That's why I had left and started a new business. Research was safe, predictable, and I didn't need a partner to work with. My only co-worker was a computer and I was pretty sure it had no plans to sleep around.

"What do you want?" I asked. "I'm kind of busy today." I looked around at the quiet office, listened to the clock ticking loudly in the silent hallway. So much for being truthful.

"It's just that I need to talk to you Hilly, I . . ."

"I don't think that is a good idea," I said cutting off his words. "We'll only drag up the past and that leads to arguments and bad feelings -- for me at least. Goodbye, Zach."

"Hilly," he shouted, "you have to listen to me. I could be dying."

I had been about to take the phone away from my ear and hang up when he blurted those words. The word "dying" stopped me cold. I may have had issues about how Zach betrayed my trust, but I had never wished him dead.

"What do you mean?" I asked. "How can you being dying? You aren't old enough. You aren't sick. You..."

"Hilly, you don't know that. You haven't seen me in a long time. Look, I need to talk to you. Can . . ."

"You can't come here," I blurted. Lamb's Bay and my father's house was my refuge. I couldn't let Zach in here -- it would destroy my little world, my comfortable little world. It would bring back all the hurt, the crying, the feelings of inadequacy.

"Hilly, you don't understand," Zach said. "Of course I can't come up there."

Thank goodness. At least he understood that.

"I'm in the hospital. They're going to operate, and then depending on the results I might have to have treatment like maybe chemo and I thought . . . I just needed to speak to you, Hilly, to ask you a favor."

"Chemo?" As I said the word an image floated in front of my eyes. My father in his last days, the wasted figure beneath the sheets, the tubes, the medications flowing in, God knew what flowing out. I hadn't wanted to know. Hadn't wanted to see my father that way. And yet, I had been forced to deal with it. Mother pleaded distance. "Lamb's Bay is so far away from where I live now, Hilly, and besides, it's expensive to travel and if, well you know, your father and I didn't part on good terms. I don't think it would be a good idea, Hilly. I'm sure you'll handle it much better than I ever could." And I had, dealt with everything. And I never wanted to do that again. And now Zach -- it was a cruel joke of some kind. It had to be.

"Hilly? Are you still there?"

Of course I was still there, my hand on the receiver held to my ear. I was standing in the office trying to absorb Zach's words. Dying was something old people, other people did. Not the man you had shared a good part of your adult life with did.

"Hilly? Hilly?" Zach's voice sounded desperate. "Are you there?"

"Yes, Zach, I'm here." Good old reliable Hilly. Capable of handling everything, even cancer. Stray cats, murdered friends, missing children, just call old Hilly and there she'd be helping and supporting. So why at the end of the day was I always left alone with the details to wrap up and no one to share my life? I took a deep breath and resumed my habitual role. "What happened, Zach? I mean, cancer? You were always so fit." So good in bed and so eager to prove it to every woman who crossed your path. "Are they sure?"

"One never knows for sure until they, they go in there, dig around, test tissues, you know all that lab stuff."

"Where?" I asked.

"Regina Mundi. You know, the same place ..." His voice trailed off. The line between us was silent.

Yes I knew Regina Mondi. Lost what could have been a baby there. Spent a long time there due to complications. Regina Mundi where they told me there could be no more children. Yes, I knew it well. I shook the images, the nightmare, out of my head.

"No Zach, I meant where is it, the cancer?"

"Oh," Zach said. "That." He began a long rambling explanation, his voice fading in and out. I was still coping with the shock of his news and didn't really absorb all the details. Images of my father's last days were swirling inside my head. Suddenly, I realized that Zach had stopped talking and that silence had fallen between us.

"Well they have to operate right away they said. I didn't ask any more details. Hilly, talk to me," Zach said. "I need to know you are still there."

I took a deep breath. "I'm here," I said. "Zach, I'm so, so sorry. I didn't know. You should have told your girlfriend Cindy to call me or at least send an e-mail."

There was a pause. Then, "Oh her. Hey, Hilly, that was a long time ago. A big mistake. She split about a year after you did. It's been just me and HD since then. That's what I wanted to talk to you about. I need someone to help take care of HD."

HD? Who the heck… Oh my god. A shiver ran through me. A child. That must be who HD was. Zach couldn't have kids with me. But with that woman... and now she had gone, been gone a long time and left him with a child to raise. A thought struck me. Did he expect...? No way. I wasn't cut out for raising kids, particularly not those created by my ex-lover and that scheming hussy.

"Zach, I'm sorry," I said. Again. "But I really don't know what I can do to help you out. I'm not a miracle worker or a super healer. The best I can offer is my good wishes and ask Pastor McCrae to put you on the prayer list this Sunday. But a kid, well, that's for family. And Zach, we stopped short of being a family. Don't you have any relatives that could help out?"

"A kid? Hilly I'm not asking you to look after a kid. What made you think that ... oh, HD."

"Yeah HD. I don't do kids, Zach. Ask your sister. She's had kids."

"Hilly," Zach said. "HD is a dog."

"A what?"

"A dog. A Golden Retriever to be exact. She's about two now and she's trained and everything. I just don't want her ending up at the pound and my cousin Tracy is allergic. She got too sick after having HD for a couple of days, so she's had to put her in a kennel. Hilly...," Zach paused. "Look I understand how you feel about me and asking you to come and see me would be really pushing it. But I need someone to help out here. If I, if I am too sick, well I don't want HD to have to go too because no one would take her in. Just for a while to see what happens to me and then if, if I'm not going to make it, could you make sure she goes to a good home. There must be someone up there in Lamb's Bay who could love HD."

A dog. My one weakness had always been animals. Zach knew that. Knew too that I'd looked after my father's spaniel Rags after dad passed. Probably guessed Rags was gone by now and good old Hilly would fall for a friendly Golden Retriever.

I sighed. I knew his sister was allergic to dogs. Knew too she was about the only family he had left. A dog. The man is about to be operated on for possible cancer and he calls me to look after his dog. As fast as the anger surged, it subsided. <u>Put yourself in his situation and what would you do?</u>

"Hilly, are you still there?"

"Yes, Zach, I'm still here. Okay, I'll look after your dog for now. Give me the details." <u>You are such a sucker, Hilly.</u> Zach dictated the name of the kennel and the phone number. I said I'd drive down that afternoon and pick the animal up. "What about your apartment while you are in hospital?" I asked and kicked myself mentally for asking.

"Locked up tight and the key is with Tracy. All HD's things, food and stuff are with Tracy too so she can give you all that and I'll write out the instructions for you and give them to her. You don't need to go to the apartment."

Thank goodness. Having to go back to the scene of our once happy life and my great disillusionment with love was not tempting.

"Great," I said. "So let the kennel and Tracy know I'll be there this afternoon around 2:30. Do you need anything else?" <u>There you go again, Hilly. You just can't leave it alone, can you?</u>

"Thanks for asking," Zach said. "I think I'm okay. I'll know more once the operation is over. I'll ask Tracy to bring you all of HD's food and toys and bedding stuff. And Hilly… "

"Yes?"

"I can't tell you how much I appreciate all this, really. I mean, after what I put you through and everything, you had every right to slam down the phone. I, I just wanted to say, I was an idiot. Can you forgive me?"

There it was, the million-dollar question. And I had no idea how to answer it. Could I, had I, did I want to forgive him for having more testosterone than brains? After all, the man was dying. Wait a minute, he said, he *could* be dying. Oh well. I sighed. Forgiveness, that's what the pastor urged us to every Sunday. I bit my lip and replied, "Zach, I, I don't know."

"Hilly, that's all right," Zach said. "I had no right to ask. Just thanks. For looking after HD. Then, perhaps some time, we can talk?"

"Yeah," I said. "Maybe. Got to get going if I want to finish some errands and make the city in time to meet Tracy at the kennel. Good-bye, for now."

A quick "good bye" and Zach was gone. I stood there for a few minutes with the phone in my hand. Then I slowly hung up and looked at the clock. I'd have to get my skates on if I wanted to get to the police station, make my statement and then get on the highway in time to meet Tracy and my new roommate.

"Who the heck calls a dog HD?" I thought as I grabbed my purse and keys and headed for my car.

Chapter 4

"So you sure you don't know this person?" Lester Spriggs asked, pushing a photo across the table to me.

I looked down at the photo of the dead woman. She didn't look particularly good but she certainly wasn't familiar either. "Honestly, Lester," I replied. "First and last time I ever saw her was when she was sprawled on the road. I don't even recognize her as someone I've seen around town. I'm guessing she wasn't a local and probably a tourist. Do you have a cause of death yet? She was soaking wet. Did she drown?"

"No, we're waiting for the autopsy results," Lester said, putting the photo back into a file in front of him. "Mind if you tell me why you happened to be on the road that early?"

"I already told one of your officers, Sid. Brody Paxton called and said he needed to me to come over asap and talk to him. He wanted to show me something." I paused. "Brody is an old friend. He sounded upset so I threw on some clothes and drove over. He's, he's been really stressed since, well since the murder and Ruby's disappearance."

"So what was so important he couldn't give you more information on the phone?"

I sighed. Brody had asked for my help in solving the murder and telling Lester at this point would just get his hackles up. I knew from experience no cop needs to know that a crime victim has asked for help from a non-cop like myself. Despite my background in investigations, Lester would consider me a civilian with no authority to look into the case. And he'd be down on Brody like a ton of bricks for talking to me instead of to the police. I didn't want to lie to Lester, but I couldn't reveal the information about Gina's research on the Paxton Point treasure without breaking Brody's confidence.

"Well?" he asked.

Lester wanted an answer so I gave him one. "He just wanted to show me some old photos of Gina and the two of us when we were kids. He's walking down memory lane and I guess he wanted to share. Plus he'd baked his famous cinnamon buns and had no one to share them with."

Lester looked at me in a way that said "riiiight!" He didn't believe me but he wasn't going to push the point right now. "Guess I should get over there and update him on the investigation," he said. "Been kind of busy around here what with two murders and all. I'll give him a call."

It was my turn to think "riiight." Lester was a decent cop, but so far his staff hadn't turned up much in the ways of clues to Gina's murder. Not to mention what had become of Ruby.

"Anything new," I asked hopefully.

"Nothing I can discuss," Lester said. "By the way, you knew Ruby pretty well didn't you?"

I wrinkled my brow. Know Ruby? "Well sure," I said. She's my goddaughter. I've known her since she was born. Why?"

"I've heard she had problems. You know about all that I expect?"

"Problems? What do you mean?" My voice rose a bit as I replied. We were all of us sensitive about Ruby. Most people didn't understand her. She had been born deaf and although she had learned to sign, she rarely talked. She also had learning disabilities and trouble getting along with strangers – which meant anyone outside of her immediate family and her teachers.

"I was just wondering, because of her, er, problems, that perhaps, well, perhaps something happened that resulted in . . ."

He didn't get a chance to finish.

"Are you suggesting that Ruby was involved in Gina's death? How dare you. She loved her mother. Lester!" My voice had definitely risen now.

Lester waved a hand at me. "No, Hilly, no. It's just that perhaps her behavior could have caused something to happen. Could Gina have intervened to protect her and . . ."
I stared at him.
"Look we have to consider everything. There's little evidence to go on. And . . . well, you know. I, we, everyone is worried." He got to his feet and cleared his throat. "Listen, forget what I said. Thanks for stopping by to give the statement. It should be ready for you to sign later today.
I stood up as well. "It will have to wait. I have an appointment this afternoon."
Lester nodded. "Okay tomorrow morning. We'll call you. You going to be around?"
"Should be." If I'm not out walking a large dog. How often did you have to walk those things anyway? Hilly get back to the matter at hand. Focus. "So can I go now?"
He nodded again and I started to walk out the door of his office.
"Oh, Hilly," Lester called.
Damn. I'd almost made it out the door. I turned back to face him.
Lester rubbed his chin and stared at me. "One thing, Hilly. I know you and Brody are old friends. You wouldn't be doing a little investigating for him would you?"
"Not at this point in time," I said. And I wasn't lying. At this point in time I was desperately trying to make my escape from Lester's office without spilling the truth.
Now if he asked me if that's what Brody wanted to see me about, I was really stuck. But he didn't.
"Okay then. Remember that's our job. And that you don't have an investigator's licence any more. But Hilly . . ."
"Yes?"
"If you do hear anything or find out anything, I'd expect you to share the information. You understand?"

Oh yes, I did. He was warning me off, yet letting me know that if Brody or anyone else let something slip, he wanted to know. That I should have him on speed dial.

"Sure," I said "Bye." I didn't give him my usual smile – after all he'd practically accused my goddaughter of causing her mother's death. It would be a while before I could smile at him and not remember his words.

I turned and made a quick departure. Outside and back in my car, I decided I had to let Brody in on the conversation. Lester might or might not follow up and drop by to see Brody and, if he did, Brody needed to be aware of what I'd said.

I looked out the windshield as I started the car and noticed Lester staring at me through his office window. He was probably watching to see if I was calling Brody. Time to move. I swung the car out of the parking lot and turned left as if I was driving home. I didn't need Lester to wonder why I was headed to Roxton. Zach's illness and his request for me to take his dog in was not cop business. I drove a few blocks to the local coffee and donut shop and parked there. I didn't need donuts after Brody's cinnamon buns, but another coffee would help. Getting up as early as I had, I could do with more caffeine. I went in and picked up a large with cream and sugar, then went and sat at one of the picnic tables outside. I took the plastic top off the coffee, but it was too hot to drink right away, so while I waited for it to cool, I phoned Brody. He didn't answer and after four rings his voice mail service kicked in. Damn. I left a quick message telling him about Lester and that I would be away for the afternoon. I'd call him this evening."

I put the top back on the coffee cup and climbed back into the car. After a quick look around to make sure the coast was clear, I turned the car in the direction of the highway to Roxton. As I drove, I forced myself to concentrate on the Zach situation rather than on the death of Gina and the disappearance of Ruby. And what changes a dog could bring into my life and whether I was willing to accept them – even if it was just until Zach recovered. If he recovered.

Traffic was light until I neared Roxton, then it got heavier and there were more trailer trucks hogging the road. However, I made good time and managed to arrive about an hour before I was scheduled to meet Tracy at the kennel. I checked out the kennel's location and then drove around looking for somewhere to eat a light lunch. It had been a while since the cinnamon buns and the extra coffee I'd consumed while driving seemed to have woken up my appetite. About three blocks south of the kennel's location I found a diner that advertised home style meals. It was located near a couple of manufacturing plants and seemed quite busy. If the workers from the nearby plants weren't keeling over with food poisoning, then I guessed it would okay for me.

The diner was pretty full and I had to take a free seat at the counter. I ordered a BLT and a soda. The noise level in the restaurant was almost mind-numbing, but I didn't bother to tune in to any of it. As I sipped my soda and munched my way through the sandwich – which was served with potato chips, my all-time favorite snack food – I thought about my years with Zach.

We'd met in college in the same prelaw program. We hated each other from the first day we talked. I thought he was opinionated and a show-off. He thought I was stuck up and a know-it-all. You guessed it. Opposites do attract and the attraction had been pretty steamy. By the time we reached graduation we were engaged and planning our future together.

Fast forward a few years and there we were, running our own security and investigations firm, specializing in the corporate field. And we were doing great. We had a wonderful home, two cars and went on tropical vacations.

It was my idea to try for a child. Zach wasn't too keen at first, but then friends of ours had their first and, despite the lack of sleep, the crying, the diapers and all the other baby-related stuff they complained about, we both realized how happy they were. Zach was good with the baby too – we babysat her a few times. So then we took the plunge.

Fast forward again to the hospital, the day after my world felt like it had come to an end. Our baby gone, the doctors telling me there were complications, that I shouldn't, couldn't have another. Sorry.

Zach and I stunned. Me, back home staring at walls, crying whenever I looked at all the baby things we'd collected in just a few short months. Zach finally made it all go away – donated it to a local women's shelter. I got help, he didn't. I worked at getting my life on track. Zach went off the tracks. He started to drink and stay out late. I was still so out of it that when I came home unexpectedly and walked in on him and his latest conquest, I had refused to believe it at first.

When I finally did, the dam broke and the anger about everything – his behavior, the treachery and, yes, the baby, had poured out of me.

Tears stung my eyes as I sat there in the diner remembering it all. The sea of voices ebbed and flowed around me as I sat there stuck in the past.

"Get you something for dessert?" The waitress' voice cut into my thoughts

"What?"

"Well, there's apple pie, tapioca pudding or Jell-O." She smiled expectantly, her pad and pencil at the ready.

"Apple pie," I croaked, "and coffee, please."

"Okay."

She sailed away and two minutes later a piece of pie and another hot steaming cup of coffee appeared in front of me. My sandwich and soda glass were whisked out of sight.

Her intrusion had stopped my voyage down memory lane and I was kind of glad. Honestly, I didn't need to go there. It had been two years, I had moved on. Or had I, given the fact that I could still feel the way I had back then? I shook myself. I had to stop this introspection.

Zach was ill. He'd asked for my help in looking after his damn dog. It was a dog. Not Zach's life. I liked dogs. Perhaps it would be a good thing. Or perhaps not. And if Zach didn't make it, I would either have a permanent roommate or I'd be stuck with finding it a new home.

The pie did look tempting. I caved and tasted it. It was very tasty apple pie. And the coffee was good, too, nice and dark. I took a deep breath, then finished off the pie and drank the last of the coffee. I paid my bill and left the diner trying desperately not to think about the past. It was almost time to meet Tracy and HD.

I also had more important things to think about. Such as Brody's concerns about Gina researching a hidden treasure and why Ruby was missing. How Gina had ended up dead and why were the police thinking Ruby had something to do with it? Life was complicated enough without adding the events of the past.

I pulled into the kennel's parking lot and there she was –
Tracy – looking as if a day had only passed since I had last
seen her. A few years older than Zach, she had always dressed
more like her mother than someone from her own generation.
Today she was wearing a blue sweater and a strand of pearls
with a straight gray skirt. Flat shoes. Matching handbag. Ultra
conservative. You wouldn't know it to look at her, but she
earned her living writing steamy romance novels, you know
the kind where the super soldier sweeps the heroine off her
feet, saves her from the bad guys and, in between, they have
lots of sex. She made good money at it. But she was very
allergic to dogs.

She ran towards me as I exited the car and flung her arms
around me. I got a big hug – these romance writers are big on
hugs.

"Hilly, darling, I am so glad to see you. Thank you so much
for agreeing to take HD. You'll love her. She's the sweetest
dog ever and . . ." She chattered on as she dragged me up the
front steps and opened the door into the reception area. "You
two will be so happy together."

"What?" I said

"You and HD."

"Oh, yes." For a moment I thought she thought I was getting
back together with Zach. She'd always liked me and when I
left because Zach betrayed me, she had kept in touch, feeding
me tidbits about Zach – that I didn't want to hear – and letting
me know she'd be so happy if we got together again. I'd tried
to dissuade her, but she would back off for a while and then
resume her gentle prodding. We were meant for each other
she always said. If we were getting back together, Tracy
would be delighted. Perhaps she thought me taking care of
HD would rekindle the spark,

Well, she was going to be sorely disappointed. I would help
out with the dog, but nothing would ever make me trust Zach
again. I could be civil to him. I could be concerned about his
illness, but take him back full-time into my life? Never.

Tracy pushed me ahead of her inside. She shouted to the receptionist. "This is the lady who will be taking HD." Then she turned back to me. "Hilly, dear, everything is arranged and Zach has prepared all the instructions. I'll call to see how things are going. but I just can't go inside the kennel. You understand."

I did. "Thanks, Tracy," I said.

"Ms. Hilly?" the receptionist said.

"Yes?" I turned towards her just as something wet licked my hand. "Here she is."

A warm body pressed against me and I looked down into two brown eyes surrounded by golden hair.

"She's ever so sweet. I am sure you'll get along with her," a second voice said.

"Huh?" I said, looking up. I hadn't realized someone was holding the animal's leash. The young vet tech handed it to me and offered to carry all the dog supplies out to the car.

HD towed me outside and across the parking lot. I steered towards my car. I noticed that Tracy was already pulling away from the kennel.

There was another tug on the leash and the next thing I knew 60 lbs. of dog was climbing into the back seat of my car while the vet tech stowed the gear in my trunk. She slammed it shut and backed off waving.

I was sitting there wondering what to do next when a thin line of drool dribbled down my neck. I looked in my rear view mirror at the furry being in my back seat. Somehow she had wedged herself so that her muzzle rested on my shoulder.

"Oh boy," I said. HD whined.

I put the car into reverse, turned it around and exited the parking lot in the direction of the highway. After a few blocks, the dog settled down on the back seat and appeared to be napping. I drove at a steady speed and took it easy all the way back to Lamb's Bay.

Chapter 5

It was late afternoon by the time I pulled into my driveway. I killed the engine and sat reflecting on my day. I reached for the coffee I'd picked up at a drive-through halfway home – it was empty. I sighed. My sigh was echoed by a whine from the backseat.

Suddenly a wet tongue caressed the back of my neck. "Cut it out HD," I said. "I'm just not that kind of girl."

I turned around and looked into a sad pair of brown eyes. The dog gave me the look. I was a sucker for that look. I reached back and fondled the dog's muzzle. What would become of the two of us, I thought. Both of us abandoned by Zach. Thrown together by the tides of fate and . . .

My god, I was getting maudlin. I yanked open the car door and got out. I let HD out of the back seat and she headed for the first patch of available grass to relieve herself. It had been a long drive and I kind of wished I could take advantage of my ragged lawn too but I was supposedly a civilized human being – I'd go inside and visit the bathroom – then come back out to get HD's baggage.

I unlocked the door and entered the front hall. HD pushed ahead of me sniffing at everything. I closed the door so she wouldn't wander out and get lost while I was in the bathroom. I was bushed and the last thing I wanted to be doing was hunting for a lost dog.

Bathroom needs taken care of, I coaxed HD into the kitchen and shut the door. Then I went out to the car and began carrying in HD's bed, food bowls, a bag of dog toys, a box of treats and finally a massive sack of kibble. It looked and smelled unappetizing and I felt sorry that the poor animal was relegated to munching down on it. However, by the way she wagged her tail when I lugged it into the kitchen, I supposed she was used to it. There was also an envelope labelled "To Hilly: HD's health records and instructions." I placed that on the counter. I'd had dogs before. I'd read the envelope's contents later if I couldn't figure things out or if HD go sick. Once everything was inside I had to decide where to put it all. Finally, I installed the food bowls in the kitchen corner on a plastic tray to protect my floor from spillage. I served HD water and bowl of her crunchy food. The treats and kibble I stashed in the pantry. The dog bed went in the corner of the kitchen for now. We'd see how that worked out.

I put a frozen dinner in the microwave to cook and poured myself a glass of wine. I settled down on the sofa with my gourmet meal on a tray and flipped on the television hoping for a little escapism. What I got was the evening news. There had been another bombing in the Middle East, a landslide further south down the coast and a mild earthquake in the Philippines. I changed channels hoping for some light entertainment. I didn't find anything uplifting so I turned the television off and finished my meal and wine in silence. Today had been brutal. Brody's call in the early hours summoning me to the point. Then finding the body on the shore road, a body I had almost run over -- the stuff of nightmares. Dealing with the police, Brody's story about treasure and betrayal and then, the icing on the cake, Zach's call. And at the end of it all, here I sat with a warm dog cuddled against my ankles – apparently HD liked me – with an empty wine glass and an urge to binge on chocolate chip cookies.

The dog rose and placed her paw on my knee. Oh boy, what had I gotten myself into?

I pushed her paw down, stood up and went to refill my wine glass. Instead of attacking the chocolate chip cookies, I wisely munched on an apple as I went into my office and sat at my desk. With everything that had gone on, I hadn't had time to go through my emails—client messages, research reports— they were all waiting for me to connect. I just didn't feel like reading them right now, so I went back to looking at the few envelopes I'd received in the morning mail. Two were bills which I put aside to handle in the morning, one was an offer from my bank for a mortgage loan at an attractive rate – I put that one through the shredder. I didn't need a mortgage and they should know that.

And then there was the odd manila envelope. It was lying face down on the desk and I turned it over. I noted again that it was addressed in block letters, but this time I saw it bore no postage stamp. It had been hand delivered. My curiosity was piqued.

With all the terror attacks in recent years there had been a lot of talk about letter bombs or letters containing anthrax spores. Law enforcement agencies had issued warnings about the dangers involved in opening unusual or unsolicited mail. I really wasn't sure about this envelope.

Should I open it? Why would anyone want to send me a letter bomb? I wasn't in the investigation business anymore. I couldn't think of any enemies who would send me anthrax spores. I did have a couple of disgruntled people in my past, but nobody who struck me as that vindictive. Or was I too trusting?

I left the envelope sitting in the middle of the desk and thought about my options. I could open it and be damned. But if it was a bomb, then both HD and I were toast. Zach would never forgive me. But did I care about that? Should I call Lester and have the bomb squad check it out – and look like an idiot when it turned out to contain something innocuous such as a flyer or perhaps an invite to a barbeque?

"Hmm, what would you do?" I asked HD. She sighed and slumped down on the floor beside me, resting her paws on her muzzle. "Some help you are," I grumbled.

I started to reach for the phone to call Lester, then hesitated. If it was nothing, he would have a great yarn to tell the other cops about crazy Hilly who over-reacted and thought she had a letter bomb. But, but . . .

I sighed and took a pair of latex gloves out of my desk drawer. I put them on and gingerly picked up the envelope again. It was a plain one, no other markings on it but the block letters with my name and address on it – and of course my fingerprints and perhaps those of the person who had left it in my mailbox.

I felt carefully all over the envelope and could not detect anything which felt like a device. All I felt was what seemed to be a sheet of paper.

"Well here we go, HD," I said. I picked up my letter opener and carefully slit the envelope open at the end. I parted the two sides of the envelope slowly and waited. No explosion. No cloud of anthrax spores so far. I took a pair of tweezers out of my desk drawer and slid them inside, secured the edge of the paper and started to slowly remove it from the envelope. Still no sign of danger. I realized I'd been holding my breath so I exhaled and then started slowly breathing again while I examined what I had removed from the envelope. It was a piece of plain white paper folded in two – a cheap brand of paper because I could kind of see through it. There appeared to be some writing on the reverse side and a dark square.

Using the tweezers, I unfolded the sheet of paper and laid it flat on the desk. It showed a blurry photo that had been printed out in black and white and below it, a message written in the same block letters scrawled on the front of the envelope. I read the words and stopped breathing again. My heart thumped in my chest. And I realized what I was seeing in the blurry photo.

It was Ruby, Ruby in clothes I did not recognize, sitting on a bench under a tree. Her eyes looked vacant. Her body language radiated fear. My lungs were demanding air. I felt dizzy and I was holding my breath again. I tried to resume normal breathing, but the message below the photo was so bizarre and threatening that I had trouble regaining control. It read: "The girl is okay. Don't try to find her. I will try to get her away. If you come after her he will kill her. Wait to hear from me." There was no signature.

With shaking hands, I reached for the phone and speed dialed Lester's number at the office. When it went to voice mail, I redialed using his private number. He picked up.

"Lester, it's Hilly."

"Hilly," Lester said. "I didn't know you had this number."

"You gave it to me last year when that stalker was bothering me."

"Oh yes and he . . . "

"Lester," I shouted down the phone. "Listen to me. You have to come to my place right now."

"Hilly, what's wrong? Can it wait until morning or would you like me to send over an officer?"

"Lester, get yourself over here now – it's about Ruby."

Lester's voice changed; it was more serious now. "Ruby, what about Ruby?"

"I got a message and a photo from her kidnappers."

"Don't move," Lester said. "I'll be there in five minutes. And he was."

Chapter 6

Lester bounded up the front steps. I was standing at the door waiting for him. I'd left the letter lying on the desk and shut HD in the kitchen.

"Where is it and how did you get it," he asked.

"On my desk and it was in my mailbox this morning."

"This morning? Why did you only call me now?" He looked angry as he barged down the hall to my office.

"Hey," I said. "With everything that happened today, I didn't get around to checking my mail until I got back from Roxton."

"What the hell were you doing in Roxton?" Lester asked as he pulled on a pair of latex gloves.

"Personal business," I mumbled.

He was leaning over the desk now examining the photo and the message. "Looks real enough. I don't recognize where Ruby is sitting, do you?"

"No," I replied. "And I've never seen those clothes on her." A tear rolled down my cheek. "Oh my God, Lester. It says they will kill her if we look for her. Poor Ruby, I'm her godmother, I've known her since she was born and …" I started to shake and cry uncontrollably.

Lester took me by the shoulders, sat me down on a chair and handed me the box of tissues from my desk. Then he pulled his cell out of his pocket and dialed.

"Harry, get over here. Got some evidence needs processing. Yeah, now." He hung up and stood there looking down at the photo.

Lester had a daughter about Ruby's age. As my tears lessened, I realized he was probably thinking how he would react if it had been his child in the photo.

"Wait a minute," Lester said. "You are her godmother, right?"

I nodded. "Yes, you know that."

"Then why would they deliver the message and photo to you and not to her father?"

"I have no idea" I said. "You're right – not that I wish such a shock on Brody, but by all logic, this should have been placed in his mailbox."

"Something's off here, Hilly," Lester said

"Do you think it's a hoax?"

"I don't think so," he replied. "Let's see what the lab can tell us. Fingerprints, etc." He turned towards me. "How did you open it and are you sure there was nothing else in the envelope?"

"I described my musings about letter bombs and anthrax attacks as well as my caution in opening the envelope using gloves and a pair of tweezers. "All I got when I pulled on the paper was that sheet with the photo and the message."

Meanwhile Lester was slowly running his fingers over the envelope. "Hilly, there's something else in here. I'm going to tip the envelope up and see what falls out. Hold another sheet of paper underneath it."

I stood by the desk and helped as Lester shook the envelope. A thin piece of cardboard slipped out, flipped and landed face up. As it fell out, I noticed there was printing on one side and handwriting on the other.

Lester and I peered at it. I went cold. I recognized it– so did Lester.

"It's your business card," he said.

"Not just my business card," I replied. "It's the one Ruby used to carry in her pocket all the time. Gina wrote their home address on the back and wrote 'godmother' on the printed side. It was in case something ever happened to Ruby, so she could show it to someone or someone could find it in her pocket and get in contact with us." I swallowed.

"Lester this is not a hoax. It is real. Very real. Whoever wrote that note was with Ruby at some point and found the card in her pocket. If they couldn't get to Brody's place, they opted for putting it in my mailbox instead." I picked up the phone. "We have to tell Brody she's alive."

Lester took the phone from my hand. "Hold on, Hilly. I want to get more information before we go getting Brody's hopes up. They could be trying to extort money and, perhaps Ruby isn't, well, you know." He didn't finish the sentence

I finished it for him. "Isn't alive anymore."

There was a knock at the door and Lester went to let Harry, one of his senior officers in. They talked in the hallway and then Harry came in carrying an evidence bag.

"Hey, Hilly," she said. "How you holding up?"

"Not sure I said, "but thanks for asking."

Harry smiled. She and I had also been at school together though she had been in the same class as my sister Vesta. Small towns are like that. Everyone knows or knows of each other.

Lester, with his gloved hands, put the envelope and its contents into the evidence bag and Harry left in a hurry. Lester turned to me. "I have a few more questions, but you look like you need some coffee. Sit down and I'll go make some. And while I do, I got a couple of calls to make. Just sit tight. Okay?"

"Okay," I said and sat back in my office chair. I felt completely at sea, not sure what the future held, worried about Ruby, worried for Brody and his sanity if it should turn out that she was dead too. And that's why I forgot about HD

A round of barks came from the kitchen and a shouted, "What the hell, Hilly?"

I jumped to my feet and ran towards the kitchen. HD, so peaceful and placid to date, had gone into protect mode in the kitchen. She was standing firm in the doorway just daring Lester to put a foot in what she now considered was her kitchen.

"When the hell did you get a dog?"

"Today," I said as I calmed the dog down and convinced her to let Lester into the kitchen. "That was my personal business."

I got HD to her bed in the corner and told her to stay. She did but kept a close eye on Lester and I as we worked together to come up with two cups of very strong coffee.

Then we went back to my office and sat there sipping. I left HD in the kitchen.

"You gonna tell me about the dog or do I have to ask?"

"It's a long story, Lester," I said. "And it has been a hell of a day."

"My wife's at her sister's and I got all night," he said, flipping open his notebook and grabbing a pen off my desk." Plus I've got questions for you. Feel like starting at the beginning?"

"Well," I said, "everything began when I found the body on the shore road and went downhill from then on."

Our conversation, mixed in with Lester's questions and my answers, went on for what seemed like a long time. Finally, Lester and his notebook went home. I let HD out of the kitchen and took her for a quick walk around the garden. She decided this would be a good time to do a number two so I had to scrounge around for a plastic bag and stoop and scoop. Then we both went inside and she had kibble while I renuked my gourmet microwave dinner. I was exhausted.

I didn't think I would be able to go to sleep what with everything that had happened today, but my body kept telling me to go to bed and I finally gave in. We both settled down, HD in the kitchen and me in my cosy bedroom.

I tried hard to fall asleep, but it took forever – possibly due to the four coffees I had consumed that day. When I finally dropped off, I had a horrible dream in which dead bodies, gangsters and oceans of blood figured prominently.

At some point, I got up and went to the bathroom. As I went back towards my bed, I heard gentle snoring. I thought I was still dreaming, but I realized I was fully awake and also that there was someone or something else in my room. I snapped on the light and raised my head almost afraid to look. I should have guessed.

There was a snoring Golden Retriever flaked out on the other side of the bed. Okay I wasn't putting up with this. She and I needed to have a serious conversation about sleeping arrangements. But right then I was too tired to deal with it, so I lay down, rolled over and went back to sleep.

Chapter 7

I didn't want to be here in this police car with Lester on my way to Paxton Point. Brody was a dear friend and we were about to bring him pain, not physical pain, but mental anguish, something no friend no human being should inflict on another.

Lester had called that morning and told me he was convinced the note and photo were real, that there were some fingerprints on the envelope and that Brody should know the current status of the case. He asked me to drive down to the police station and ride along with him to the point. He said he hoped having me there would help Brody deal with the situation.

I really didn't want to be part of this visit, but I also knew that Brody needed to come clean to Lester about Gina's work on the treasure file and what bearing it could have on the case. I had to find a way to get a moment alone with Brody to convince him of that.

It was mid-morning and the gulls and pelicans were flying around the bay down near the wharf where the local fishermen sold their catch. We drove past the area and turned onto the shore road which lead to the point.

Lester was not in a talkative mood and neither was I. We'd already discussed the situation on the phone when he had called earlier to tell me he was coming to pick me up to go to Brody's. I knew I was being used as a buffer, as the sympathetic voice, the "there, there" person who would make coffee and listen to Brody's grief. That was a role Lester had no interest in fulfilling, though he had been very kind to me the night before when I had found the envelope with the photo, note and threatening message.

We turned onto the road that lead out to the point and the lighthouse. As we neared the cottage, I thought about memories, all the happy times I had spent out here with Gina and Brody – both when the three of us were children and later when Gina married Brody and Ruby came along.

Now we were about to deliver another blow to a man already reeling from the grief of his wife's death.

Brody saw the car before it was even halfway to the cottage and was waiting for us outside the door. I could see by his face as we drove up that he had steeled himself to accept the worst news possible. He thought we'd found Ruby's body. In reality, the news was worse. Ruby was being held somewhere. And we had no idea where.

"Morning, Lester, Hilly," Brody said. "Coffee?"

Lester shook his head. "No thanks. I've had enough today I think. Can we talk inside?"

"Sure." Brody led the way into the cottage's cosy living room and motioned for us to make ourselves comfortable. We sat down and Lester began talking

"Brody, we've had a development in the case. And we wanted to share what we have with you."

"You found Ruby's body, didn't you," Brody said, his eyes lighting up with anger. "Those bastards killed her like they killed my Gina." He shot to his feet and began pacing the room, his hands punctuating his speech.

"No, no," Lester said. "Brody, stop that pacing, sit down and listen to me."

Brody stopped and turned to Lester. "What, then?" He slumped into a nearby armchair.

Lester pulled a photo out of the folder he was carrying. My heart stopped. Was he going to show him what I had received in the envelope? I was about to protest, when I realized he was showing Brody a photo of the dead girl I had almost run over on the beach road.

"Right now, I'd like to ask you if you know this woman or if you have ever seen her before," Lester said.

"Why me?" Brody asked defensively.

"Not just you Brody. We have officers showing this photo around the town and I thought I'd check with you as well. We don't know if the two cases, Gina's and hers, are connected, but we need to identify her. Have a look please."

Brody grabbed the photo out of Lester's hand. He stared at it long and hard, then shook his head. "Doesn't ring any bells. I am sure I never saw her. Do you really think her death and Gina's are connected?"

"We have no idea right now, but two murders in the same area in one week seems odd. Anyhow thank you for taking a look."

"And you still say you don't know her either, Hilly?"

"No," I said. "Do we know yet how did she died?"

"Looks like she was hit on the head and held down in the sea. That's the preliminary finding. So it is murder."

"So that's it?" Brody asked. "Nothing else new?" He jumped up and resumed his pacing. "I wish I knew what happened. I can hardly deal with losing Gina because I'm so upset about Ruby."

Lester stood up and grabbed Brody's hands as he strode by. " Brody, sit down and listen. We have other information to share."

Brody didn't sit but he stopped pacing and stood in front of Lester. Lester cleared his throat. "The other news is that we now have a note with a photo of Ruby, left anonymously by one of the kidnappers."

"A note? A photo? Found where? Is it ransom they want? I'm not rich but I'll sell everything if it will get my Ruby back. How much do they want? Tell me man. Tell me." He reached out and shook Lester by the shoulders.

"Calm down," Lester said. He pulled Brody's hands away and stepped back. "And listen to me or I'm leaving."

Brody eyed the two of us, then resumed his place in the armchair.

"There was no demand for ransom. Just a note saying Ruby was okay and this unknown person was going to try and get her away. And that they'd be in touch, but no name and no way to contact that person."

"How did you get this note," Brody asked.

"Well, actually Hilly got it."

"Hilly? Why Hilly? I'm her father and . . . "

"Take it easy, Brody. We found Hilly's business card in the envelope along with the note and the photo – you know the card Ruby always carried with her?"

"Yeah, I know about it," Brody said. "Gina thought it would be a good idea for Ruby to have it in her pocket so someone could contact us or Hilly if she was lost or in trouble. But . . ."

"But nothing," Lester said. "We don't know why that person left the note at Hilly's. Perhaps he couldn't get out to the point and thought it was easier to leave it at Hilly's. Also Hilly lives in an area with lots of trees so there's less risk of being seen leaving the envelope in her mailbox. Out here on the point, there aren't any trees and you can see people coming the moment they head in this direction. That's the only explanation we've come up with so far."

"I see" Brody said, nodding. "I guess that makes sense. Thank god, Ruby had that card on her so they could get the note to us. When did you get it, Hilly?" He turned to me.

I'd been silent up to that point, letting Lester do his job and bracing myself for providing Brody with support when the reality of the situation sank in. I was also trying to figure out how to get Lester out of the house for a few minutes so I could talk to Brody about divulging the information about Gina's obsession with the treasure myth.

"It was placed in my mailbox at some point," I said. I didn't go into details about the delay between delivery and me looking at the note. I didn't want Brody to be upset thinking that he had been prevented from knowing earlier that his daughter was alive. "I found it in with my mail when I got back from Roxton yesterday."

"Roxton? Yesterday?" Brody swung round and looked at Lester. "Why am I only hearing about this now?" He looked back at me. "Why didn't you call me last night? Hilly, you're my friend."

"Hey," Lester said. "We had to make sure it was authentic. It could have been a hoax. Don't dump on Hilly. She wanted to call you last night and I asked her to wait until we'd had a chance to check it out. The lab's working on some fingerprints we found and they are trying to see if they can find anything else that might help us in finding Ruby."

Brody's shoulders sagged. "Sorry. I understand. I shouldn't have yelled, it's just that." He put a hand up and swept his hair back from his brow. A ray of sunshine coming through the curtain bathed his face in light and I suddenly realized that my friend had aged in the days since Gina had died and Ruby had disappeared. He looked sallow and haggard, his clothes were rumpled as if he had slept in them and he had beard stubble. Brody had never been one for beard stubble. He had always prided himself on being neat and tidy. Now he and his clothes looked worn out.

Lester got up. "We'll contact you if we get more information. Please bear with us. It is a difficult case and we are doing our best."

"I know, I know," Brody said. "Is there anything at all I can do? Anything?"

Here was my chance. "Lester," I said. "Could you step out for a moment?"

Lester stared at me. "What?"

"Please just step out for a few moments. Please. Trust me?"

Lester wrinkled his brow. "Okay, a few minutes. Got to check with the dispatcher anyway." He left and the front door banged shut. He wasn't happy and he didn't understand my request but he was going along with it. Thank goodness.

"Hilly?" Brody stared at me.

"Brody," I said, "you have to come clean about Gina's obsession with the treasure story and the file that she had put together. I think you are right. It does have something to do with what happened to Gina and Ruby. It's important evidence. I know you didn't tell the police before because you were angry that the investigation seemed to be going nowhere. I told you I will do some research for you to see what I can find out. But Lester and his staff need that information as well. Will you please tell him and agree that I can give him a copy of the file? It might just help to break this case wide open."

Brody sank into an armchair. He put his head between his hands and sat quietly. I thought he was thinking, but then I saw his shoulders were shaking and I knew he was crying. I grabbed a box of tissues, then went over and knelt beside him and put my arms around him. He raised his tear-stained face to mine. "Okay," he said. "Get Lester in here but give me a moment."

He stood up, wiping away the tears, and went down the hall into the bathroom. I heard the water running. He was probably washing his face with cold water, I thought as I walked to the front door to call Lester back into the cottage.

To put it mildly, Lester was ticked off about Brody not telling him before about the file he had found. But he held the anger in and listened patiently to Brody.

"That file is where now?" he asked.

"At my place," I replied. "I'll bring it to you."

Lester gave me a hard look. "All of it?" he asked.

"All of it," I replied.

Lester stood up. "Okay. Brody I'm sorry this all happened, but perhaps this information about treasure hunters will give us some new leads."

Lester's cell began ringing. He excused himself to go and answer it in the hallway.

"Brody," I said. "Thank you."

He nodded. "You are right. It was foolish of me not to let the police know. But I was so mad that they weren't getting anywhere."

"It's a complicated case," I said. We could hear the rumble of Lester's voice out in the hallway. "Let the police do their work. And Brody?"

"Yes?"

"Listen, as one friend to another, you don't look like you are doing so well. You're out here alone on the point. Why don't you go and stay with your sister Debbie or even at my place? Or I can come by more often if you wish? You shouldn't be alone at this time.

Brody shook his head. "I have to stay here. What if Ruby comes home and I'm not here. I'm staying put. But Hilly, you are right. I don't think I am doing so well." He sighed. "I'll try to do better, but I'm not sure I know how."

"At least take a shower, change your clothes, ~~and~~ make sure you eat and get some sleep." I made a mental note to let Debbie know that Brody could do with some attention and some home cooking.

He gave me weak smile. "Okay, mom. I promise." The smile faded. "Do you really think Ruby is alive and this, this person can free her? That she'll come home alive?"

"Shush, Brody," I said. I patted his arm. "Don't go there. One day at a time."

"Yeah," he said just as Lester came back into the room.

"Gotta go," Lester said. "They need me down at the station. Come on Hilly, time to roll. Bye Brody. We'll keep you posted." He headed down the hall towards the door. I gave Brody a quick hug and followed Lester out to the Jeep.

To Brody, Lester had expressed his anger about not knowing about Gina's file in a fairly diplomatic manner. That was not the case once the two of us were in his car and heading back to the station.

"I do not appreciate you withholding evidence from me, Hilly," he said. "How could you? You call me about a suspicious note and yet you were hiding potentially crucial information from me. I thought we were friends. You know I hate it when amateurs think they can solve police cases."

"Sorry," I said. "But in my defence, Brody swore me to secrecy. And I did get him to tell you about it.

Lester actually harrumphed.

"I promise it won't happen again," I said.

The rest of the drive back to the station was quiet. Lester was sulking and I didn't want to say anything that might set him off on a rant about amateur detectives, one of his favorite pet peeves.

"I promise I'll be back in an hour or so with the file," I said. "I have to walk the dog."

"You'd better be or I'm sending a squad car out there. And Hilly?"

"Yes," I said

"The dog? What gives?"

"I'll explain when I have more time. See you shortly," I said as I ran over and climbed into my own car, slamming the door shut. I pulled out of the parking lot and headed back home fervently hoping that HD hadn't had any accidents or temper tantrums while I was out because I'd left her shut in the kitchen. I'd walked her for over half an hour this morning and expected that she would sleep most of the morning.

When I got home, I went through the gate into the back yard and in by the back kitchen door. HD appeared to be glad to see me, but even happier to head for the open door. I followed her out into the garden and let her ramble around doing her business and exploring my bushes while I munched on a granola bar. I lured her back inside with a treat and then went into my office and picked up Gina's file.

I was cutting it fine, but I figured I had just enough time to get to the do-it-yourself copy shop and make a duplicate of the file's contents. I had promised to comply with Lester's request that I hand it over. I'd made no promise about doing a little research myself.

At the copy shop, I commandeered a machine and started frantically feeding the papers from the file into it. They ranged from printouts to old clippings and there was even an old notebook that appeared to be a diary of some kind. I didn't have time to absorb any of the information. I concentrated on getting it all copied so I could read it later so didn't pay much attention to any of the words. After all I could take my time reading everything later today.

An hour later I walked into the station and asked for Lester. Marge the receptionist/dispatcher gave me a wan smile. "He's asked me three times if you'd called. Seems he's been calling your house and not getting an answer. Last time he asked me, he told me he was giving you 15 more minutes and then he was heading out to your place."

"Well, here I am," I said.

"And it's about time," Lester said as he walked down the hall from his office.

He stood there with his hands on his hips, frowning at me. "What took you so long?"

"As I said, I had to walk the dog and I had lunch and a client called." I smiled as sweetly as I could and held out the file. "Here it is."

"Thank you," he said. "Bring it down to my office."

I followed Lester into his office expecting another tongue-lashing, but instead he wanted to ask me more about the file. "What do you think, Hilly? Did Gina ever talk to you about this stuff?" He was flipping through the clippings and printouts that Gina had collected. "I vaguely remember some yarn about gold buried on the point that my grandfather talked about, but he said it was pirate gold."

"I don't remember ever hearing anything about it," I said. But Brody told me all about it. Said Gina had hidden the file in her bedside table drawer and he found it by chance. He said his family had run off treasure hunters a few times over the years and wondered if it had anything to do with Gina's murder and Ruby's disappearance."

"And he asked you to look into it? So what did you find?"

"Honestly, Lester, I never had a chance to look it over. That day, when I got home, I was going to read it, but I got a call and had to go into Roxton on personal business. When I got home, I was too tired so I figured I would look at it in the morning, but then I found the envelope with the note containing the photo of Ruby and called you. I just never got around to examining it."

Which was true. While I had copied everything in the file, I hadn't yet had a chance to read any of it. I'd take care of that task this afternoon.

"And Gina never mentioned this whole treasure story to you? You were best friends."

"I know. I was as surprised as you, but I guess she just wanted to keep it to herself for some reason. And we'll never know why she did that."

The phone rang. Lester ignored it.

It rang again. He looked at it and then back at me.

"I'd better get this. Look, keep in touch, okay?"

"Sure thing" I said, making a hasty retreat out the door. Once back in my car I drove home, stopping only to pick up a frozen pizza for my dinner later on. Back at the house, I stashed the pizza in the freezer, put on a pot of coffee and then made a quick call to Debbie to fill her in on Brody's condition. She thanked me and said she would check on him, deliver some home-cooked food and "might even get him to come over here and stay instead of moping out on the point by himself." As she hung up, I whispered "good luck with that one." I knew Brody would not want to leave the point – he was waiting for Ruby to find her way home.

I poured myself a coffee then armed with a full mug, I curled up on the sofa to read the contents of Gina's file.

Chapter 8

The road to hell is paved with good intentions. My good intention to digest the Gina file, as I was now calling it, was seriously derailed over the next couple of hours.

The first interruption came from a client who had been waiting for some material I should have emailed him two days ago. But instead, I'd found myself involved in a murder investigation as well as Zach's news about his illness. I apologized sincerely, citing a family illness and quickly assembled the material into my standard report format and sent it off to him.

My second disruption was a call from Tracy. I almost didn't pick up, thinking I could call her back that evening, but curiosity got the better of me.

"Hi Hilly, how's life with HD?" Tracy sounded just as chipper as she had been when I'd seen her a couple of days ago.

You'd think she'd be a little more subdued considering Zach's illness I thought. Then I apologized silently to her for being so petty. We all handle adversity differently. As I remembered, the worse things got, the perkier and more chipper Tracy got. Given her current level, I braced for the worst.

"Fine so far," I said, keeping my voice even. "Nice of you to inquire. The dog seems to like me but I find it strange that she doesn't seem to be missing Zach at all."

"Maybe it was the stay in the kennel," Tracy said. "The staff said she would just mope and not eat. Maybe she thinks she was abandoned."

"Well, she's eating, here," I replied.

"I knew she would be better off with you," Tracy said.

There was an awkward silence between us. The unspoken question hung there and I couldn't stand the suspense. I dove in headfirst. "How's Zach?"

"Well, um," Tracy said, "we won't know till after the operation. It's scheduled for tomorrow afternoon now. I guess you are wondering how long you will be stuck with HD but I can't even tell you how long he will be in the hospital and whether he'll be well enough to look after her. I think he'll have some restrictions on mobility. I'll keep you posted. Are you planning to be away or anything?"

"No, none for the moment."

"Great," Tracy replied. "Well, I won't keep you. Take care."

"Wait, Tracy." But the line went dead

I sat there listening to the dial tone. I'd missed my chance to ask the questions eating away at the back of my brain. What the heck kind of a name for a dog was HD and what did it stand for? Shaking my head I hung up the phone. I wanted to get back to sorting through the file in front of me.

Tracy's call, however, had stirred up a mixture of emotions. Was there something she wasn't telling me? Or was I overreacting? It sounded like I'd be babysitting HD a lot longer than the few days Zach had mentioned. To be fair, he had asked that I find her a home if he didn't make it and I decided I didn't want to keep the dog. I looked down at the golden dog huddled on the mat beside me. Almost as if she knew what I was thinking, she raised her head and gave me that look again. The look that said "Look after me." I sighed and patted her head.

Good old Hilly – a sucker for sob stories be they delivered by men or dogs. And that line of thinking got me to worrying about Brody and his current state. At least I'd let Debbie know how badly he was doing and she was now looking out for him. But he needed more than just Debbie's home cooking. He needed a friend to support him. And I knew I would be that person. Especially if the worst came true and we lost Ruby. Even if | Ruby was found and brought home, she would have issues due to the trauma she had suffered and he'd need help there and I was her godmother.

<u>Wow</u>. Here I was a couple of days ago thinking how glad I was to be on my own and responsible for no one and now Zach is hovering on the edge of my life, his dog has moved into my home and my best friend's husband needed my support. Life can change in the blink of any eye.

I really had to get back to sorting through the file and try to make sense of it. I forced myself to focus finally and reopened the folder.

Gina had amassed a mixture of old clippings and printouts from the Internet. There were also notes written in Gina's hand which made my eyes tear up for a minute. I knew that writing so well. I guessed the notes were information she'd looked up at the library or somewhere else.

I was trying to make sense of the order when at the bottom of the pile I found the copies of the small notebook which had been in the original file. I had been so intent on making copies and getting the file to Lester, I hadn't really looked at it then. Now that I examined it closely, I could see it was not in Gina's handwriting. The name on the inside cover was that of Brody's grandmother, Christine Paxton, the woman who Brody had told me about a few days ago, the woman who had actually experienced the events which took place when the bank robbers came to Paxton Point.

Chrissie had kept a diary of her daily life, but about halfway through the narrative changed from mundane matters such as laundry to a written account of what really happened that day. Somehow Gina had come into possession of it. She probably found it among Brody's grandmother's things in the attic at Paxton Point or perhaps the woman had spoken to her about it and then given her notebook for safekeeping. No wonder Gina was so obsessed with the story.

I sat there reading the long forgotten words of how Chrissie and her husband had been terrorized by the robbers. She had also included notes about what happened in the days afterwards when the police came. And of how the point was searched and she and her husband were questioned. The officers were convinced she and Myron knew where the gold was stashed and the two of them had been extremely upset by the allegation. They were the ones who had been attacked and who had found their nephew's body in a pool of blood.

One entry read: "Myron is furious and I am so upset. How could these men think we were in on the robbery and know where the gold is? I am so mad at them that even if I found it, I wouldn't tell them where it was. It is cursed and it can rot wherever it lies. No good can come from that so-called treasure."

A few later entries mentioned Chrissie and Myron chasing off treasure hunters convinced they could find what the police and FBI couldn't.

"These men are desperate for the gold," Chrissie had written. "Thank goodness Myron taught me to use a rifle – I've had to fire off a few warning shots to chase away idiots in boats who want to comb the caves below the lighthouse looking for the gold. Others have come to the house brazen as all get out. Luckily we can see them coming down the point and we are armed and ready to chase them away. My concern is at night – I just can't sleep so I've taken to spending the nights up at the light with Myron. There I can sleep without worrying that some idiot will come in the night, break in and try to force me to tell them where the gold is. I wish I did know where it was – then I would give it back to the bank so that life on Paxton Point could return to normal."

Poor Chrissie. She was so traumatized by Dan's brutality and his murder of Elwood that she couldn't even sleep in her own bed at night. I shuddered. I never wanted to know how that felt. I loved my cosy safe house and, despite noises in the night from wind, creaky old beams and rainstorms, I never worried about someone coming to attack me. When I shut the door at night, I felt safe.

Most of the clippings in the file were old and I suspected that Chrissie had saved them, particularly the ones about Dan's escape attempts and of how both times he was headed for their part of the coast when apprehended.

Some reporter had done a splashy story on Dan's death. Of how he had been gunned down trying to rob a bank and had hung on in the hospital for several days out of his head on painkillers. Brody had said the man never gave up any information to the police. But Gina or her grandmother had underlined a paragraph in the story that said Dan's sister Doreen had visited him several times. She always maintained he never told her anything. But there was speculation she knew something.

Gina had put a stickie note at the bottom of the clipping. She'd written "she claimed she knew nothing but did she really? Or did he tell her something because of the drugs and she didn't realize what he had told her. Perhaps?"

I put the notebook and clippings down. I was tired and cramped from sitting so long.

I looked at HD. "Time for a walk," I said. She thumped her tail. So off we went.

I walked down my driveway and out onto the road. As I cut through a group of scrub pine that bordered my lot, I thought I heard something. I know HD did. She stopped and growled. Something in the way one of the tree branches moved didn't fit the harmony of the other branches.

"Hello?" I called. "Is someone there?"

The only answer was the sound of footsteps that faded into the wind. Kids, I thought. My neighbours two houses down had four boys who were always wandering around in the woods playing games. Still I should look into it?

HD and I cautiously approached the place where I thought I'd seen something. I whipped the branch back and of course there was no one there. But when I looked down I saw footprints in the damp earth – adult footprints. Someone had been there – a grownup not kids. I scanned the area. Whoever it had been was gone now. I worried that perhaps they had been watching to see when I left the house.

I turned around and headed home at a good clip. HD wasn't a fan of our swift return but kept pace with me. Back at the house, I walked around the building and checked that no doors or windows had been tampered with. Outside the window to my office I noticed the bushes had been disturbed and there were two footprints like the ones I had seen in the woods. Someone had been looking through that window at some point and I hoped it wasn't when I was sitting with my back to it. It gave me a creepy feeling.

Why would someone be checking out my house or watching what I was doing? Perhaps it had been the person who delivered the envelope? Or did we have a peeping tom in the neighborhood? Whatever the case, I didn't like the situation. I let HD loose in the back yard, pulled out my cell and called Lester. I wasn't taking any chances with my safety.

Lester was out on another case so they sent Harry in the squad car. She checked things out and promised to have a patrol car pass every hour tonight. I nodded but I wasn't that convinced. An hourly patrol was a nice idea but it is easy to track. It was the 59 minutes in between patrols that worried me.

After supper that night, I took HD for her last walk around the property. She didn't growl or seem to find anything of interest. Once we were both back inside, I checked every window and door lock. I closed all of the curtains so no one could look in. And I put the Gina file into my office safe. I had no idea if the intruder had something to do with that case, but I wasn't taking any chances by leaving the material lying around.

Before I closed the safe, I took out my gun. I didn't really like guns but sometimes they were a necessary deterrent. I was all set to go up to bed, gun in hand when I looked down at HD who was hovering at the foot of the stairs.

I'd been so wrapped up in the events of what was going on that my intention of having her sleep in the kitchen at night had fallen by the wayside and it was obvious she planned to grace the other side of my bed each night she was with me. She cocked her head, wagged her tail and started up the stairs. I put out the downstairs lights and followed her. I shook my head. I'd have to adjust to sleeping alone again after she went back to Zach, if she went back to Zach.

"One day at a time," I mumbled as I got ready for bed. HD was already curled up on her side. Making sure the gun's safety was on, I placed it on my bedside table where I could easily reach it. I settled down and started to read a new novel I'd bought a few days ago.

I was definitely tired and I dozed off with the bedside table light on. I would have slept that way all night if HD hadn't suddenly erupted in a volley of barks and leaped off the bed. My eyes shot open. I could HD barking like crazy downstairs and some thumps and bumps and a man's voice swearing at her.

I grabbed my cell and my gun. I pressed the speed dial for 911 on my phone and started towards the hallway, gun at the ready. I snapped on the light, illuminating the scene in the downstairs foyer. HD stood in the hallway growling and barking at a hooded stranger holding a gun who was taking aim at her. Seeing the lights come on, he whirled around and bid a hasty retreat to the back of the house and the kitchen where the door led out into the garden. HD gave chase.

I ran down the stairs, shouting into my phone at the same time. "Help intruder," and giving my name and address.

I ran into the kitchen and found the back open door. The man must have fled into the night as I could hear HD still barking and growling out in the garden. Suddenly there was a shot and then silence.

"Oh, no, no, no," I screamed. I ran out onto the back porch, visions of a badly wounded animal in my head. Luckily the intruder was not a good shot. He'd managed to fire a shot that went wild and just nicked HD's left ear. Blood was oozing from the scrape and she was whining.

I tugged on her collar and got her back into the house just as a squad car, siren blazing, pulled into my driveway. Someone pounded on my front door. I left my gun on the kitchen table and pulled a terrified HD behind me by her collar as I went to answer it. It was Harry and her partner Sid.

"A man," I gasped. "Broke in. Shot my dog. He ran out the back."

Harry called for backup while Sid went to search the garden. I was cuddling a shaking HD now, her blood soaking into my nightgown. I heard Harry tell the dispatcher "and we need the emergency vet too."

"Yes we do," I said, "and a shot of whisky wouldn't be out of line."

"For the dog?" Harry asked.

"No, for me, for me," I replied.

It seemed like hours but it wasn't that long before the emergency vet and more police arrived at the house. The vet checked out HD and decided to take her to his surgery to sew up the injury to her ear. I helped him get her into his car, then turned to talk to Lester who had just arrived. He had plenty of questions, starting with whose gun was lying on the kitchen table.

By the time I had answered his questions and he had left, it was after 2 a.m. My nightgown was ruined due to the bloodstains, so I took a quick shower and changed into a fresh one. I tried going back to bed, but I couldn't sleep even though Lester left an officer to guard the house overnight. The police had taken my gun away to check if it had been fired and HD was having her ear sewn up. I was all alone except for the officer on guard duty. Now I knew how Chrissie had felt after Dan's attack.

My so safe home I had been so smug about had been violated. I wasn't usually as spooked as I felt, but reading Chrissie's diary had sparked my imagination. And the shooter who had wounded a poor innocent dog just trying to do what she felt was her job had showed me that I was dealing with someone who had no scruples and probably no humanity.

I wrapped myself in my robe and went downstairs again. I got a shot of whiskey into me and then made coffee, strong coffee. I needed find out why the man had broken into my house. What did he want? Was he just a burglar or was he after the file? It must have something to do with the anonymous message left in my mailbox. But what? I wracked my brain and drank too much coffee.

I removed Gina's file from the safe, reread the diary and began to go through the printouts and clippings. I needed to find some answers as soon as possible. Gina was dead. Ruby was missing and now HD had been injured trying to protect me. This had to stop.

Chapter 9

Lester and dawn arrived at about the same time – unfortunately I had dozed off looking through Gina's file and the photocopies were spread all over my desk. My brain was still asleep – the only reason why I didn't get Gina's file papers out of sight in time

Lester appeared in my study armed with two coffees and a bag of breakfast sandwiches. He put down the bag and cups and started to move the papers so he could give me my breakfast. Suddenly he realized what the papers he was moving were all about.

"What the hell? Hilly?"

My brain clicked into gear. "Oh god," I blurted. "Sorry, Lester, really I'm sorry."

"You went and photocopied the file before you gave it to me? After I specifically told you to hand it over and not to consider trying any amateur detective work? Hilly come on."

"I said I was sorry," I said weakly. I was bleary-eyed and not convincing.

"I don't know what to do about you, Hilly," Lester grumbled as he handed me my coffee. "Here I am worried about you. I come over with breakfast to check on you and you are doing exactly what I asked you not to do – looking into the case."

"I'm not really," I said. "Honestly." I took a big gulp of the coffee. "It is just that Brody asked me to read the file and give me his opinion as to why Gina was so interested in the story. That's all I'm doing. Scout's Honour."

Lester handed me a breakfast sandwich. "Hilly, that's a crock. We all know you would never have been a Scout – they didn't let girls in. Girl Guide?" he asked with a semi-hopeful tone.

"Uh, no, never joined. Sorry again."

Lester reached for his own coffee and swallowed a mouthful. "So. What you got?"

"Huh," I said, through a mouthful of English muffin, egg and sausage.

"I said what have you discovered, what do you think? Is the file pertinent?"

I swallowed my mouthful of food and washed it down with some of the coffee. "Yes, good stuff."

"The file?"

"No, the sandwich." I cocked my head. "Just kidding. Of course I meant the file. Have you read it all?"

Lester harrumphed. "Between my police work and being called out to deal with your problems on a regular basis these last couple of days I've only had time to leaf through it."

"Okay." I reached for the photocopies. "Read this while I finish this food. I'm famished." I handed him the copies of the diary.

For the next while the only sounds were coffee sipping and me crumpling the left over sandwich wrappings and tossing them into the garbage. I sat back in my chair and slowly drank my coffee while waiting for Lester to finish reading.

He finally looked up at me. "This is pretty interesting stuff. I mean the account of the attack by this fellow Dan. And other stuff she wrote in here. Plus all the clippings.

But why was Gina so obsessed by it all?"

"Chrissie was Brody's grandmother," I said. "I expect she talked to Gina about it and either gave her the file or Gina found it when the grandmother passed away"

"It's a compelling story and perhaps there had been someone looking for the treasure when she was young and now someone else was looking. It makes sense that she would haul out this old material and follow up with some online research. I just wish she had asked me to help her out. After all research is my business."

"Well, you know Gina – she probably thought you were busy and she didn't want to involve you in it until she was surer of her facts. Did she ever mention she might be writing a book about? There are a lot of notes in here."

I shook my head. "No she never mentioned writing anything. But she was good at that sort of thing. Gina did a historical book for the library when Lamb's Bay celebrated its 200th birthday a couple years aback. This would make a good story. But she never mentioned a thing to me or Brody and, when she worked on the other projects for the birthday celebrations we knew all about it. She even had me digging up information on the shady Captain Amos Lamb, who settled here in the early 1800s."

"Yeah, I remember hearing about that in school. Didn't he use another name and buy a farm to settle down on. But finally someone gave him away and he was arrested? Funny when you think of it, that the so-called upstanding citizens of the time would use his name for the town."

"Actually," I said, "that's not why it is called Lamb's Bay – there used to be a rocky outcropping at the head of the entrance to the bay that looked like a sheep's head."

"Really? I never remember seeing that."

"Earth tremor about 100 years ago," I replied. "Some of the rocks toppled off the cliff into the water and the similarity to a sheep disappeared. The cliffs around here are always unstable, you know that. Why even parts of Paxton Point have fallen off and changed the shoreline."

"Yeah," Lester said. "That's true. Hmm. I always thought the place was named after the captain."

Lester seemed to be in a calmer mood now than when he had found the photocopies on my desk. So I took a deep breath and plunged ahead.

"So, going back to what you asked, yes I think there is something to this file. I didn't see any indication of secret hiding places on the point, but perhaps the killer or killers thought there were."

I emptied my coffee cup. "If Gina was asking around about this story and an interested party found out, they might think she was trying to find the gold instead of just following up on the information in the grandmother's diary entries. That may be what this is all about."

Lester put his empty coffee cup on the desk. "Hilly, I tend to agree with you. But we still have no idea who these bastards are and why they would kill Gina, throw her off the cliff at the end of the point and take Ruby."

I've thought about that," I said. "Right now I've got a possible scenario."

"Let's hear it."

"Perhaps these, let's call them bad guys, went to the point when Brody was away. Gina could have been down by the cliffs at the lighthouse. They found Gina and tried to force her to tell where the gold was." I paused.

"Then Ruby, who was always near her mother, heard them yelling and came to see what was going on. So the killers grabbed Ruby and said they would hurt her if Gina didn't tell. That would make Gina fighting mad. Perhaps she attacked them and told Ruby to run. She was pretty feisty. In the fight, she falls and is knocked unconscious. Her attackers panicked and pushed her off the cliff."

"Then what?" Lester asked. "And why take Ruby?"

"The killers panicked, Ruby had seen everything. But they hadn't planned on killing anyone. They left taking Ruby with them, thinking she could help them find the gold. But they soon realized she couldn't. Perhaps the thieves fell out over what to do with Ruby. It seems that way since the anonymous note mentioned trying to get Ruby away from him – presumable the guy who organized the whole operation. And perhaps . . . wait a minute."

"What?" Lester said.

"That woman. The one I found dead on the shore road. Maybe we aren't looking for a man who dropped off that note. Perhaps it was a woman and the bad guy had come after her and killed her. Remember I told you I saw a dune buggy fleeing down the beach when I stopped to get out of my car?"

"That would make sense. As you say, perhaps this isn't two cases, it's one. Good thinking, Hilly. I'll put more resources on finding that dune buggy. Locals might own one but outsiders would have to rent or steal one. I hope we find out who that woman was. That would give us a direction to look in. I'll get after the lab. They should have had a report on that envelope by now."

He stood up and turned to go.

"Oh, by the way, the locksmith will be here this morning. Jenkins Locks."

"Locksmith – I don't need a locksmith."

"Yes, you do," Lester said. "That front door lock is easier to get through than day-old bread. And the rest of the locks on this place aren't much better. I bet you never even thought about someone possibly getting in through the old root cellar door out behind the house."

"Er, no," I said. "It's padlocked."

"Yeah, with a rusted padlock that could be broken in two minutes. You are getting new locks. The bill is coming to me so I have proof they were put in – you can pay me back later. Now go to bed, Hilly. You look like hell."

"Not tired," I said. "This food and coffee have given me a second wind. I'm going to get dressed and have another go at the contents of this file. Plus I have some client work to do."

Lester gave me a hard stare. "Don't be a hero. Hilly. I don't want to hear you've collapsed or something."

"I won't, "I said. "Get out of here, Lester."

"I'm going," he said. "There's still an officer guarding the house until we have more information or some leads on what went on here last night. Oh, and I almost forgot."

"Yes?"

"The vet called and said your dog is fine, just a scratch really, but it bled a lot. She's got a couple of stitches but she'll be fine. You can pick her up after lunch."

"HD," I said. I felt really guilty. I'd been so busy working on Gina's file and possible scenarios for the murders that I'd forgotten to follow up with the vet.

"Huh?" Lester replied.

"HD, that's her name."

"HD? What the hell kind of name is that for a dog? And Hilly, you still haven't told me why you decided to get a dog."

"I didn't decide," I replied. "I'm looking after her for an old friend."

"How old?"

"Ex-boyfriend."

"That creep Zach who cheated on you?" Lester frowned at me. I sighed and wished I'd never told Lester the whole sad story.

"Yeah, he called. Lester, he probably has cancer. He's being operated on today."

Lester snorted. "Serves him right after the way he treated you."

"I understand how you feel and I have to admit that thought passed through my mind, but you have to think of the animal."

"Really? The dog or Zach? And couldn't someone else help out?"

"His sister is allergic to dogs and he was worried about the dog pining away in the kennel. He didn't want her to be unhappy so he asked me to look after her for now and if he doesn't well, you know, make it then to either keep her or find a good home for her."

"Hilly, I like you but you are such a pushover sometimes. I mean, couldn't his girlfriend, the fabulous Sandy take care of the dog?"

"Cindy, her name was Cindy," I said. "And no, they aren't together anymore."

"She left him – after all he put you through so he could move in with her?"

"Yeah and he was lonely so he got a dog."

"Well if that don't beat all," Lester said. He chuckled. "And you fell for that story?"

"I know, I know, but you saw her. Could you leave an animal with those amazing brown eyes in a kennel to pine away?"

Lester chuckled again. "Well it's a good thing she was here last night to chase off that intruder. I think you better keep her around for a while. By the way, what does HD stand for? Did he name his dog after his cable television service?"

"I doubt it," I replied. "Zach can be odd at times, but I don't see him doing something like that. It must mean something. She's purebred so perhaps the breeder gave her some weird name and Zach just uses the initials because he finds her real name embarrassing. Like me – I hate Hilaria, but I'm okay with Hilly."

Lester looked even more amused. "Oh, so do you think he asked the dog what she would prefer?"

"Lester," I said. "I'm warning you."

He smiled. "Keep that dog around, Hilly I think you two are perfect for each other and you do need a bodyguard." He walked out of the room and I threw a pencil at his retreating back. "Sometimes, Lester," I mumbled, "sometimes . . ."

I reassembled the contents of Gina's file. At least I had won that battle. I'd been worried Lester would be so upset at my amateur detective effort that he would take all the photocopies away with him.

I got dressed just in time for the locksmith to turn up. I had never changed the locks on the house since I inherited it from my father. As I was no longer in the investigation business, I hadn't thought about having a security system.

The locksmith, Brad Jenkins, inspected my doors and windows and the doors to the old root cellar. He tut tutted to himself like an old granny. In fact, I found him quite judgmental about the state of my locks. While he inspected them, he delivered a pedantic lecture about safety and deadbolts. Bottom line was that my house was like Swiss cheese.

He finished his assessment, went out to his van parked in my driveway and came back with an assortment of tools and some boxes containing new locks. He went to work and I left him to it.

I just wanted him to be finished so that I could go and get HD at the vet. Lester had said she would be ready for pickup this afternoon, but for some reason I was anxious and would have gone right away if it hadn't been for Mr. Jenkins and his toolbox.

It was afternoon by the time the new locks were all installed. I was swallowing a peanut butter sandwich and a glass of cold milk when Mr. Jenkins ambled into the kitchen and presented me with two key rings containing keys with colour-coded tops. He asked me to follow him and proceeded to explain which key was for which door.

He'd been thorough, even coming up with a serious-looking lock for the root cellar doors. I tried to remember his instructions and was wondering if I should get some notepaper and a pen when he handed me a small colour-coded card on which he had put the necessary information about the keys.

Just as he finished, his cell buzzed. He looked down at it and said, "Oh gotta go. Good luck." As he drove away, I looked down at the card and hefted the key sets in my hand. I would need to do some homework to try and remember which key went where and I sincerely hoped I wouldn't lose the explanatory card. Or lose the new keys and find myself stranded outside my old house.

I got ready to go and get HD. I placed a soft blanket on the back seat with one of her toys. I put her leash in my purse along with a dog treat. I replaced my old house keys with the new set, put them in my purse and went out to the car.

It was only when I started driving down the road that I remembered Lester had omitted to give me back my gun.

Chapter 10

At the vet's, I sat in the waiting room with an annoying yappy Chihuahua and his owner, a nervous young woman who kept telling him to be a good boy. Although the other woman had been there when I arrived, the receptionist called me in first. Followed by grumpy looks from the young woman and the yapping of the ridiculous dog, I walked down the hall to an examining room. Inside, the room smelled of antiseptic and dog kibble. I was getting used to the dog kibble smell at home, since I smelled it every time I fed HD, but I'd never gotten used to the smell of antiseptic – at a vet's or at a hospital. I always associated it with wounds and infections. I tried sniffing my jacket lapel instead hoping there was still a trace of my spring flowers fabric softener left in it, but no such luck. The door opened and HD came into the room with the vet, who introduced himself as Dr. Simons. The dog was wearing a plastic cone round her neck and she came right over to me wagging her tail. I bent down and hugged her being careful not to touch the bandage on her ear or the cone.

"How is she," I asked the vet.

"Pretty good – she has a couple of stitches and I gave her an antibiotic shot just in case. Has she had all her regular shots? Need any boosters?"

"Um, I don't know," I said standing up. "I'm looking after her while a friend is in hospital. He arranged for all her things to be given to me but, oh wait, there was an envelope marked instructions and health record – I guess that information would be in there."

"You didn't look?" the vet asked, raising an eyebrow.

"I've had a dog before you know. My dad's dog. It's not that complicated. "

"Well, no, but sometimes an animal has certain needs and it always good to know the status of their shots. Call us when you get back if you can and just let us know so we can put it in her file. In case something else happens while she is visiting with you."

"Okay," I said. "I'll do that. Any special instructions?"

"The nurse will give you all that and explain the medication. It wasn't a deep wound and should heal fairly fast. But she should keep the cone on for now so she doesn't scratch it as it begins to heal. Sometimes healing scars feel itchy."

"Got that," I said. "But how can she eat with that thing on?"

"You could try taking it off when you feed her, but you'll have to sit with her to make sure she doesn't worry that wound. Or you could put her bowl on a small step stool so she doesn't have to bend down. You'll figure it out between the two of you. I'll see you in a week to take out the stitches."

"Will the cone come off then?"

"No, we like them to keep it on a little longer so they don't scratch. Off you go – see the receptionist and the nurse on the way out."

I exited the examining room letting HD lead the way. There was no room for two of us to go through the door with that cone round her neck.

In the reception area, the nurse met us, explained the medication and the receptionist handed me the bill and asked if it would be cash or credit.

After I recovered from the shock of the bill, I handed her my credit card. Wow. I had forgotten vets could be so expensive and I guess there was an extra charge on that bill somewhere for coming out in the middle of the night.

As we made our way to the car, I told HD, "No more getting shot at. Next time, let me do the shooting."

HD didn't seem to hear me. She was having too much trouble trying to get into the car with her cone on. Between the two of us, we managed but every time she swung her head in the back seat to look out the window I got whacked on the back of the head by the plastic cone. I was not looking forward to the next couple of weeks with a conehead dog. Maybe Zach would get miraculously well and take over from me. Faint hope, I thought.

Just then my cell rang. I saw it was Lester so I pulled into the supermarket lot and parked so I could answer.

"Hey, Hilly, we got a lead. I thought you might like to ride along."

"Seriously?" What had happened to the "no amateur detectives" speech he had given me – twice in the last couple of days?

"Yeah. A woman who owns cottages and a motel down in Fair Haven reported missing guests a couple of days or so. One was a woman."

"The body on the beach road" I blurted.

"Could be. Anyhow Harry, Sid and I are going to see her and I thought you might come up with some ideas or questions. You up for it?"

I looked back at HD. It was almost time for one of her painkillers which the nurse had said would make her sleepy.

"Good timing, Lester," I said. "just taking HD home. And then I can come."

"How is she?"

"Fine, but she has to wear this annoying cone until everything heals."

Lester laughed. "Been through that when the cat got into a fight. It was enough of a pain, but with a dog the size of HD – you're going to have fun. She'll be knocking everything over. I suggest you stash your valuables."

"Yeah, sure," I replied. Actually he was right. Perhaps HD could take care of some of those ugly Edwardian-style figurines my grandmother had collected. I kept them in memory of her, but I really hated them. I made a mental note to make sure they sat on the coffee table. Couldn't blame me then could you, Nana, if the dog did it?

"Hilly, are you still there?"

I'd gone off daydreaming again. I really was tired after everything that had happened these last couple of days.

"I'm here. I'll drop HD off, make sure she swallows her meds and perhaps she'll sleep all afternoon."

"Oh Hilly, is that worry about the dog that I hear in your voice?" Lester's voice dripped with sarcasm. "She's got you really good."

"Leave me alone, Lester, unless you want to come and help me get a large dog to swallow a pill."

"Uh, no thanks," Lester said. "I'll give you 20 minutes or so. Want coffee?"

"Yes and a doughnut with chocolate sprinkles."

"That's not good for you," Lester replied.

"According to the Internet, neither is coffee."

Lester laughed. "Okay, see you soon." He hung up. I noted that he sounded in a good mood and I hoped the lead, whatever it was would advance the investigation. We needed to find Ruby and identify the dead woman as well as the people who killed both her and Gina.

Back at home, I managed to get HD to swallow the pill by wrapping it in a piece of ham. Then she retired to her bed and lay there looking forlorn. Obviously she didn't understand the whole cone business and wasn't too happy about it. That made two of us.

I went to the counter and looked for the envelope that had accompanied HD and her food, etc. It had been pushed to the back and the coffee can was sitting on it. I brushed off some loose coffee grounds and sat down at the kitchen table. Inside was a copy of HD's health record which showed her shots and boosters. I put that aside to email to the vet. There was a list of instructions written in a handwriting very familiar to me – Zach's. I pushed aside my resentment of him and forced myself to read his notes, concentrating on what they told me about taking care of HD.

By the end of the sheet of paper, I was pretty sure I was doing a fine job of babysitting my canine visitor.

There was, however, a second sheet of paper just listing some of her favorite snacks other than the ones that had been provided. Then, halfway down, there was a note addressed to me from Zach.

"Hi Hilly. Thank you so much for taking care of HD. I know you two will get along just fine and this prevents me from worrying about her while I am in the hospital. Hope to be out and see you both soon. Regards Zach"

See me soon – I hoped not. I didn't wish dying or a prolonged hospital stay on him, but I had no need to meet with him for any reason. When the time came for HD to go home, I planned to drop her off – no standing around reliving the good old times.

The note was written on Zach's office stationary. Wait a minute – on the phone he told me he had written out the instructions in the hospital. So when did he add the note to me?

Then it struck me – he didn't add it after he spoke to me on the phone. This had been his plan all along – to cajole me into offering to help a former lover in need of a dog sitter. The conniving creep. I wasn't suspicious before because I knew Tracy was severely allergic to dogs and I had never thought to question how long HD had been at the kennel. I threw the note on the floor and stamped on it. HD raised her head and woofed.

"Calm down," I said. Your owner is a creep. Perhaps he is not even sick. Could that be true? On one hand, I could not see Tracy agreeing to some crazy plan of Zach's to get me to look after his dog so he could see me. Or would she? It was just the kind of situation that would appeal to a romance writer. And she had told me a couple of times how sad she was when the two of us broke up because she had always thought of us as the perfect couple.

I was about to launch into a string of curse words when I heard the squad car pull into the driveway. HD rose to her feet, but I told her to sit which she did, despite a low growl in her chest. I shut the kitchen door so she couldn't get out, grabbed my purse and left the house.

In the car. Lester handed me a chocolate sprinkled doughnut. A cup of coffee sat in one cup holder and he drove while sipping from the other.

"How come you look so pissed?" Lester asked.

"It's personal."

"Must involve Zach and that damn dog of his," Lester said.

"Something like that," I replied, biting into the doughnut so I didn't have to say any more.

Lester cleared his throat and sipped some more coffee. "Nice day for a drive."

I nodded and we both remained silent for the short drive to nearby Fair Haven.

A small picturesque village a bit further down the coast, Fair Haven boasted a marina and several tourist cottages and motels. It was a quiet town so the tourists were mainly families or people who wanted more privacy. It would have been a perfect place to stay for the bad guys who had killed Gina and taken Ruby.

As we headed down the main street, Lester spoke. "Seems two men and a woman – said they were brothers and a sister – rented one of these cottages. They paid in advance for a week and the owner said they appeared to have diving equipment in their SUV – she noticed it through the windows. She did not see them much and they were very quiet. After the week was up, they didn't come to her office to return the keys, so she went over there. When no one answered, she went inside. There was some luggage lying around, the place was a mess and the keys were lying on the dresser. No sign of the diving equipment or the SUV. But she did say some of the stuff left behind was female-oriented. I thought it was worth looking into."

Lester drove into the parking lot of the Fair Haven Cosy Motel and Cottages. Harry and Sid had arrived ahead of us and stood talking to a mid-thirties woman wearing too-tight jeans and a stretchy top that was straining to do its job properly. Man, oh man," Lester said as we got out of the car.

Chapter 11

The woman made a beeline for Lester. "You the one in charge?" she asked.

"That would be me," Lester replied.

"Who's she?"

"Miss Barton-Cheswick is a consultant with our police department."

Her gaze took in my conservative shirt and black pants, my usual working outfit. She didn't appear to approve of my outfit and turned to focus her attention on Lester. After all he was the man in charge.

"I'm Daisy Unger. I own this place. And those people stiffed me. What are you going to do about it?"

"Well, ma'am, as I understand it they paid in advance, right?"

"Right."

"In full?"

"Yeah."

"So they didn't stiff you, but they did leave without telling you."

The woman shrugged. "Technically that's true, but," she added, pointing a finger at Lester's chest, "they had no right to take off and leave that cottage in a mess. It took me and my daughter a couple hours to get it ready for the next renters."

Lester stepped away from her finger. "So someone else is already staying in the cottage? And you've cleaned it?"

"Yeah, so what?"

"Well, not much chance of us finding any useful fingerprints now is there?" He looked at her intently. "You should have called us sooner and not disturbed anything. What did you do with their things?"

"What I always do with stuff people leave behind. I tag it with the room number and put it in a bag in my storage place. If they don't come back or call me within a couple of weeks, I sell what I can."

"Must be an interesting sideline," Lester said.

The woman glared at him. "I am not a thief. I'm an honest person. You can ask anyone. Why I even tried to call those people, but the phone numbers and address they gave me turned out to be bogus. Then when I saw the woman at the gas station a day or two ago . . ."

"Wait a minute." Lester said cutting through her flow of words. "You saw the woman recently? After these people had left your place?"

"Yeah. I was getting gas when a blue sedan pulled in beside me. I looked over and it was the woman who had been staying here. I rolled down the window and shouted to her. 'I got the stuff you guys left in your rooms. Come by the office and I'll give it to you.' They left a few nice things behind."

"What did the woman do? Did she recognize you?"

"You bet she did," Daisy said. "Her face changed, she put the car in gear and shot out of the gas station area as fast as she could go. Almost hit a red pickup truck."

"And she didn't come to see you and get the items they left here?"

"No. Kept an eye out for her all day, but she never showed."

Lester took a breath then asked "Ms. Unger, can you describe this woman?"

"Dark hair, good looking, didn't appear to wear much makeup. Nice body. Expensive jeans. Wore gold earrings – hoops they were."

Lester motioned to Harry and she came over with an envelope. He pulled out a photo and handed it to Lester.

"You know this woman?" Lester showed Daisy the photo.

"Oh my god," Daisy said. "Oh my, is she, is she dead?"

'I'm afraid so." Lester put the photo back in the envelope and handed it back to Harry.

"That's her," Daisy said, "but she looked better alive. Oh my goodness I need a drink."

"I'll need to take the things they left in the room. It's evidence," Lester said. "And we have questions. Can we talk inside? Hot afternoon."

"Oh yes, yes." Daisy ushered us all into her cramped office and we perched on cheap folding chairs.

"Cassie," she yelled. "Cassie, come here."

A teenage girl appeared in the doorway. "These people would like a drink, I am sure. You mind you bring the good Scotch."

"Wait, ma'am," Lester said. "We're on duty." He smiled at the girl. "A glass of water each would be just fine. And Cassie, did you help your mother clean out the cottage?" Cassie nodded. "Then we'll need to talk to you, too."

Cassie turned to go.

"Water maybe fine for you," Daisy said, "but after seeing a shocking photo like that I need a Scotch. Make sure it's the good stuff Cassie."

Lester and Harry took out their notebooks. "So, from the beginning, Ms. Unger. When did these people arrive and can you describe the two men with this woman?"

Cassie edged into the room and handed her mother a substantial Scotch. Daisy took a healthy swallow. "Both kind of ordinary looking, clean shaven, athletic, dark hair. One had a silver earring."

"Left or right ear?"

"Don't remember. And the other one always wore a fancy watch, one of those you know you can dive in."

"Okay anything else. Accents?" She shook her head and had another mouthful of Scotch.

"What address did they give?"

Daisy leaned forward and grabbed the register off her desk and read the address out to them. "153 Elm Drive, Lathorne. Telephone number was 555-621-4545. Car license 234 G78."

"We'll try tracing the car licence. You called that phone number?"

"It is out of service," Daisy said.

"And the address?"

"I have a friend in Lathorne – asked her to drive by the place."

"And?"

"It's an abandoned factory."

"Hmm," Lester mumbled. Then he cleared his throat. "So did you notice anything unusual about them? You said they told you they were brothers and a sister?"

"Yeah, but they sure didn't act that way," Daisy said, sipping more Scotch. The taller one, the blonde . . ."

"I thought you said they both had dark hair."

Oh well, one had very dark hair and the other one was blonder, you know that kind of blondish brown hair that people get when they are in sea water a lot?"

"Uhuh," Lester said. "You said they didn't act like brothers and sister?"

"The blonde one always seemed – when I saw them which wasn't often, I do respect my guest's privacy – anyway he was always kinda like flirting with the woman. But she wasn't buying it. I could tell by her body language." Daisy was down to the bottom of her glass of Scotch. "Cassie," she shouted, "I need a refill."

Lester, Harry and I exchanged glances. Clearly Daisy had a drinking issue. We had to keep her focused before the booze made her sleepy.

"And the other man?" Lester asked.

"Sort of kept to himself. Where is that girl? Cassie?"

Lester carried on his questioning. "And how often did you actually see any of them?"

"When they were outside or perhaps a couple times when I was changing the beds or cleaning and walked by their cottage. They never closed the curtains – well, they finally did on the last day I saw them."

Obviously Daisy was a motel owner with a penchant for spying on her guests.

"He was so rude, the blonder guy, he gave me a dirty look as I passed by and ripped those curtains shut. With a lot of force. Tore one of the curtain hooks out of the material. And I have to pay for that to be fixed since they took off like that."

Just then Cassie tiptoed in with a tray of water glasses and handed them out to us. She had also brought along another Scotch for her mother. As Cassie started to leave the room, Lester motioned for her to stay.

"Anything else?"

Daisy took a hefty swig of her Scotch. "Well, there was a lot of diving equipment. The SUV – it was dark green – had a roof rack and I saw them taking scuba tanks off and taking them inside the first day they arrived. After that they weren't around much during the day. Of course, I couldn't tell at night unless their lights were on."

"So, bottom line, they were here a few days then they didn't come back."

"They left in a real hurry," Cassie said suddenly.

"They did? You saw them," Daisy asked.

"Yeah, I was coming home from visiting a friend and saw them all getting into their SUV. It tore by me—I think it was the third day they were here. Almost ran me over."

"You never mentioned that," Daisy said.

"Um, I was supposed to be cleaning out one of the cottages. I was trying to get back without you seeing me."

"And now you tell the police you saw those people leave and you didn't tell your own mother?"

"Got to tell the truth to the police," Cassie said, smiling sweetly in Sid's direction. Sid blushed. Oh boy.

"Yes, you do and that's helpful information, miss" Lester said. "So all three of them got into the car and left."

"Three?" Cassie wrinkled her brow. "I'm sure I saw four people. Two men and two women – well a girl and a woman."

"You saw a girl with them? She wasn't with them when they checked in was she?"

"I don't know," Cassie replied. "Mum checked them in."

"I only saw the three of them when they rented the cottage," Daisy said.

Lester, Harry and I looked at each other. This was the first hint of where Ruby could have gone to. If they had killed Gina and taken Ruby, then at least she had been alive when they left Fair Haven. The licence plate Daisy had given us could be legitimate in which case the police could track down the SUV. But we all knew that there was a very good chance both car and license plate had been stolen.

"Anything else you need to know?" Daisy asked. "I do have a business to run."

"Just a couple more questions," Lester said. "So you waited until the week was up and rerented the cottage?"

"They paid for a week. I was fair and left things as they were. But it is the beginning of tourist season and I'm pretty well booked up. I had a family of four due in there right after them. I had to clean up and get it ready."

"Other than the ripped curtain hook was there any other damage?"

"No, just a mess of things on the floor. Which as I said are in my storage shed in a bag."

"Cassie, anything to add?"

Cassie went red and fumbled behind her neck with two hands. "Just this." She produced a thin chain with a small medal on it. "I, I found it when I was checking out the dresser drawers to make sure they were all empty. I'm sorry. I should have told but then she might have sold it," Cassie said defiantly looking at her mother. "And I wanted something pretty for myself for a change."

"Cassie Unger." Daisy had lurched to her feet and was reaching for the necklace. Lester beat her to it.

"Ms Unger, leave her be. She's doing the right thing giving it to us." Harry held out an evidence bag and Lester dropped the necklace into it.

"I watch television crime shows," Cassie said. "I'm sorry, but I washed it after I found it so there probably aren't any fingerprints on it."

"Why did you wash it?" Lester asked.

"It was covered in dried sand. I guess she dropped it on the beach, put it aside to clean and then forgot it. It was pretty," she added longingly, "and I just wanted something pretty."

"I am so sorry, officer," Daisy said. "That girl."

It's Chief," Lester replied. "And she just might have given us a real clue so please give her a hard time." He smiled at Cassie. "Girls like pretty things."

Cassie smiled smugly at her mother who swallowed half her tumbler of Scotch in one gulp. She looked angry. I didn't want to be in Cassie's shoes when we left.

"The things they left behind?" Lester asked.

"Yeah this way," Daisy said. She grabbed a set of keys and stomped out of the office.

Cassie beat a hasty retreat to the other room as we followed Daisy out into the parking lot. She led us across to her storage unit which turned out to be a rundown garden shed with plastic shelves inside. There was an assortment of plastic bags in there.

"I thought you said you sell or donate the stuff you find," Lester said.

"I do" Daisy said, "but with all the tourists in town I haven't had much time to dispose of these things."

"Yeah," said Lester, scanning the half empty parking lot. "Looks real busy to me. So where's the stuff those people left behind?"

Daisy pulled a large green garbage bag off one shelf. It had a number on it.

"See? I number the bags so if anyone comes looking for things, I can give them back. I'm an honest woman you know."

"Uh huh," Lester said. He pulled on a pair of latex gloves and so did Harry. Gingerly, Lester opened the bag and looked inside.

"Underwear, clothes, some running shoes, oh wait a minute, looks like a purse." Lester reached in and removed a black leather shoulder bag. He opened it and looked inside. Empty. "Was there anything in here when you found this?"

"Of course not," Daisy said.

No money, no credit cards, nothing? We can check on the cards you know."

"No nothing."

"Well, there's something in that little back zipper pocket," he said. He eased the zipper open and removed a small cardboard square. "A business card. Hmm."

I was curious but knew better than to ask about the card in front of the woman. I'd ask Lester later and hope he gave me the information.

Harry put the purse and card into evidence bags. Lester checked out the bag some more and found only more underwear and a diving mask with a broken strap.

"Oh," Daisy said, "I remember something."

Lester looked at her while I admired his patience. The woman was so annoying I had an urge to shake the information out of her, but then I calmed myself and thought perhaps, given the amount of Scotch she drank, information only filtered through to her brain in dribs and drabs.

'What," Lester asked.

"The first day they were here one of the men asked if there was a shop nearby that sold face masks. He wanted to go snorkeling."

"And you told him?"

"Shelby's the hardware store. Sells lots of stuff like that. Must have found what he wanted because there was a Shelby's bag in their garbage can."

"Their garbage? Do you still have that?"

"Er, no," Daisy said. "Pickup was a few days ago. I don't like to keep guests' garbage around – there's usually all kinds of weird stuff in there, if you know what I mean."

"Uh huh," Lester intoned. He gave the big bag to Sid and told Harry to get back to the station and send it to the lab as soon as possible.

As Harry drove away, Lester, Daisy and I strolled back to his car.

Lester handed her a business card.

"Now, Ms. Unger, if you remember anything else or Cassie does, I want you to call. Tell them it's the case of the murdered woman found on the beach road and the receptionist will put you through to one of my officers or myself right away."

"Sure thing," Daisy said. "Anything for you, officer."

"Chief," Lester said.

"Chief," she replied, fluttering her eyelashes.

I wanted to laugh but instead I turned and headed for the car. Daisy continued flirting with Lester all the way to the driver's door of his car. He said goodbye to her and got in. I was already in the passenger side trying not to laugh. Good god, the woman was something else and I didn't really want to know what.

As Lester pulled out of the parking lot, he said, "What's eating you?"

"Oh that woman, she spies on her guests and probably steals from them. And the drinking and the flirting."

"Hey, takes all kinds," Lester said.

"You like that kind?" I asked.

"No, that's why I married Maureen."

"Oh, of course."

"She gave us some good info even thought we had to drag it out of her. And I hope that necklace proves helpful." He snorted. "That poor girl wanting something pretty and not knowing it probably belonged to a murdered woman."

"I feel sorry for her," I said. "I bet Cassie is getting told off by her mother right now."

"Nah," Lester said. "While we were checking out the bag of stuff left in the cottage, I saw her come out of the office, hop on a bicycle and take off down the road. She'll wait till her mother has drunk herself to sleep before she returns tonight."

"That's so sad, Lester."

"Yeah, it is."

We drove in silence for a while and then I casually asked Lester what was on the business card.

He cleared his throat and said "you know better than to ask that, Hilly. We'll check it out and, if it is relevant and we think you need to know, I'll tell you."

"Sure," I replied.

To change the topic, he said, "I need more fuel for me, not the car. You want more coffee?" Lester pulled off the road into a cafe parking lot.

"You don't have to ask," I replied. "Hi, my name is Hilly and I'm a coffee addict."

Lester chuckled. "Let's go."

We went into the café, sat in a booth and ordered two coffees. The place was pretty quiet at this time of the day so we could talk without fear of being overhead.

"Hilly," Lester said. "You know I don't approve of amateur detectives, but you've been somewhat helpful on this case."

"Gee thanks," I said between sips. "I like to be somewhat helpful."

"Don't make fun, Hilly. I'm trying to give you a compliment."

"Thank you" I said more graciously. "And thanks for making me a consultant," I added. "Does that title come with a stipend? Benefits?"

"Only the satisfaction you get from helping us nab the bad guys," he replied. "And free coffee down at the station."

"Throw in donuts and it's a deal," I replied.

"Done," Lester said and we shook on it.

"You know, Hilly, I've been meaning to ask you something."

"What's that?"

"You ever miss the investigation business? After all you were in it for some years before you, before you and what's his name broke up and you moved back to Lamb's Bay to live with your dad."

"Zach," I said. "His name is Zach. And yes, I do miss it at times. Trying to figure out a puzzle and the satisfaction you get when you can help your client out. But we started out helping people and Zach pushed and shoved the business in the direction of corporate work. I didn't really enjoy that as much."

"If I helped a woman out with her divorce or a man with a custody battle, I felt like I had accomplished something good. But how can you feel good about giant pharmaceutical firms. And don't get me started on working for lawyers. They are just plain evil – well not all of them, but the ones in the cutthroat corporate sector are. They pay well and our company was doing good business, but I no longer enjoyed the game, the hunt." I drank some more coffee.

"When Cindy snared Zach, I was still reeling from losing the baby. I was getting psychological help and focusing on the business as much as possible. Zach wouldn't see a shrink. Claimed they were all nuts themselves. But he took out his frustration by not only acting out, but acting out with another woman."

"You said they broke up?" Lester asked as the waitress brought the bill.

"That's what he told me when he called me about taking care of the dog."

"Uh huh," Lester said. "And you sure he's really as sick as he says he is? I mean this could all be a ruse to get back in your good books and reconnect with you."

My shoulders slumped. "I thought of that."

"When?"

"This morning." I told Lester about finding the note at the end of the dog instructions.

"He must have written that before he went into the hospital and dropped the dog off at the kennel with her belongings. He knew I was a sucker and I'd take HD. And I don't even know why that lovely animal has such a stupid name."

"Why don't you ask Tracy? Isn't she supposed to call you to give you an update on Zach?"

"Yeah, the operation – I used the two fingers of each hand to signify air quotes –was supposed to be this afternoon."

"You could call the hospital and find out if he's even a patient there."

"I would have thought of that," I shot back. "But you came knocking at my door for our jaunt to Fair Haven."

"Well, try it when you get home."

"What if they put me through to him? I don't want to talk to him?

Lester reached across the table and patted my arm. "If he was supposed to have an operation this afternoon, he won't be taking any calls for a while And if he does answer, well there's your chance to ask him."

"Ask him what?"

"What the dog's stupid name means and if he really is in for an operation and whether he has cancer."

I shook my head. "Lester, I just don't want to talk to him at all."

"Hilly, it's been my experience that . . . "

"I don't' want to hear about your experience," I said petulantly. "Let's go. I have to walk and feed his dog." I swallowed the rest of my coffee and was about to rise when Lester reached out and caught my wrist

"Hilly, you and I have known each other since grade school. You were always the smart girl in class. I may not be the brainiest person in the world, but I do know that nothing comes of ignoring a situation. You have to face it and deal with it."

"I did – I left Zach and moved back to Lamb's Bay."

"You moved away and let him take the condo plus everything else. He lived there with Sandy."

"He bought me out of my half of the business," I said. "And the woman's name is Cindy."

"It doesn't matter what her name was. You should have fought harder for your share of the condo and not let him get away with it. And you are doing it again. Getting sucked in by those little brown eyes on the dog and thinking you are only helping the dog when in reality you are doing something for Zach, He's manipulating you."

Lester was right and I knew it. I had to find out if Zach was really ill and I shouldn't be afraid to confront him if he was pulling a scam just to get in contact with me.

"Yeah, Lester. Thanks." I said. "Perhaps Tracy has already called. I'll speak to her first. I really can't see her getting involved in a scam, but she did always say she was sorry we broke up. You know those romance writers."

"Ah, not personally, but I've heard." Lester put the tip on the table for the waitress and rose to his feet.

"What? How?"

"Stuff. My wife reads them."

"Oh," I said. "I was beginning to think you were a cop with some interesting reading habits."

Lester threw back his head and laughed. "Don't you dare start a rumour like that around the station house," he said. "Come on, it's getting late and you have a sick dog to feed. Let's get going."

"Don't push it, Lester," I said.

He smiled and followed me out to the car. We headed down the road towards Lamb's Bay. Lester had given me a lot to think about. I'd start with talking to Tracy, then check things out at the hospital. I needed to know the truth.

Chapter 12

I got out of the car in front of my house. A glance at my watch told me HD probably needed a walk about now. As I shut the car door, Lester rolled the window down, leaned out and handed me a box.

"What's this?" I asked

"Your gun. It's been cleared of an attempted assault on a canine." Lester smiled. "No charges will be filed against it or you."

"Your idea of a cop joke?" I asked, taking the box from Lester. He snorted. "Oh Hilly, loosen up, will ya?"

"I've just got a lot on my mind right now. And I want to speak to Tracy and the hospital to find out if Zach really is ill and that this isn't a ploy for him to contact me."

"Just don't use that gun on him if he is putting one over on you."

I gave Lester a baleful look. "I'm not that stupid."

"No you aren't. Anyhow keep it close. I know you got new locks and that and I kind of feel good knowing you have a temporary canine advance warning system. Wish you'd consider an electronic alarm system. I've suggested it before."

"No way," I said. "I hate those things. They make me nervous. If you mispunch the code, they go whacko on you. I think I'll stay with the new locks and HD for the time being."

"Suit yourself," Lester said, "but be careful. Keep your eyes open when you are walking the dog. And if anything weird happens, call 911."

"Lester, you are beginning to sound like my mother."

Lester smiled. "Everyone needs a mother, Hilly. Even me."

"Bye Lester," I said forcefully. Tucking the gun box under my arm, I pulled out my new keys. I tried to remember which one opened the front door, gave up and pulled my little colour-coded card out of my purse. I found the right key and let myself inside.

As I turned to shut the door, I noticed Lester was still watching from the squad car. I waved and shut the door. Honestly he was such an old granny sometimes but, in a way, I liked the fact that someone was watching my back. Lester had been a good friend all through my school years and it was nice to know I still had a friend like him.

HD was not happy. The cone of shame was driving her nuts. She banged around the kitchen in it as she found her way to the back door and whined. I let her out into the back yard to relieve herself. Then I decided a long walk along the dunes would be good for both of us.

I loaded HD into the car, no mean feat with that damn plastic cone attached to her head, and drove out to the beach near Paxton Point. There were a few tourists on the beach, but no one objected to HD and me walking along. In fact, she garnered quite a bit of attention and a lot of "poor doggie" comments from the tourists.

One woman asked me how she hurt her ear – was she attacked by another dog?

"No, she got shot chasing a burglar," I said.

The woman looked shocked.

What kind of world do we live in when people shoot dogs?" she asked her husband. The couple oohed and aahed over HD and she lapped up the attention. She's a real diva, I thought. Who knew Zach, the centre of attention in his own world, would end up with a diva dog?

I bid the tourists good bye and we continued down the beach. As we neared the section where Brody's rental cottages were, I saw him come out of the rental office, get into his car and drive off. Well, at least he was leaving the house now. I hoped Debbie and her caring ways would help him heal as the days went by.

When HD and I returned home, I found a message on my machine. It was from Tracy. I sighed. "Here we go," I told HD. The big news – is it real or fake? HD ignored me and continued to lap water out of a bowl I had placed on a footstool. It was just the right height for her to reach with the cone around her head.

I decided to listen to the message while seated at my desk. "Hi, Hilly," Tracy said. "Guess you and HD are out roaming the dunes or something. Anyhow Zach had his surgery and the doctor says it looks good, but he has to stay in the hospital for a couple of days. He's not to have visitors right away the nurse said, but I'll let you know when you can drop by and see him. I hope everything will heal well and that Zach and HD can go home soon. You must find HD a lot of work since you aren't used to looking after someone. Hugs."

The message ended.

Tracy's perkiness offended me as did her words. Not used to looking after someone? I'd spent a whole year caring for my father during his last illness. I'd cared for his dog Rags until he was too old and blind and had to be put to sleep – one of the hardest decisions I'd ever had to make. Obviously Tracy didn't know much about my life post-Zach.

As for that comment about dropping by to visit him, what was that all about? Like hell I was going to drive to Roxton to see that man. If he was really ill, then I had compassion for him but I would never allow him to take over my life again.

As for HD going home soon – well, somehow I found that a sad idea. I'd been apprehensive when I agreed to take her in, but she was doing a good job of working her way into my heart.

The hospital. I'd planned to check that Zach was really there. I knew I was being somewhat paranoid about this whole situation, but experience in my years with Zach had taught me that he was perfectly capable of manipulating events to suit himself. Asking me to care for HD could just be the tip of the iceberg. What did he plan next? Well, it wasn't going to work. I looked up the number of the hospital online and called. I pressed "3" to get patient information and asked if Mr. Zach Mayfair was still a patient there.

A receptionist told me that he was but that he was not taking any calls until the next day. "It's room 6513 – if you call back tomorrow and dial that local you'll get directly to him," she told me.

I thanked her and hung up. So he really was in the hospital. There had been no use asking the receptionist what was wrong with him. They would only give that information out to next of kin so I had to trust what he and Tracy had told me. Or did I? In retrospect, there had been a dearth of details about what kind of cancer he was supposed to have, etc.

"Take it easy, Hilly," I told myself. "But much as I like her, HD goes home the minute he's out of hospital and no, I won't be visiting him."

I picked up Gina's file which was lying on my desk. I'd neglected to put it in my safe while I was out. Luckily there hadn't been another attempted break-in. I was pretty sure that the burglar had been after that file, but why?

The information Gina had put together was in the public domain. Anyone could get it online — except of course for the notebook written by Chrissie — but there hadn't been anything like a treasure map in it. Just a recounting of the facts.

Perhaps there was something missing from the file. Printouts could have fallen out of the file into the back of the drawer it was found in.

Printouts? The penny dropped. I did not remember seeing a printer at Brody's house. I knew he had an older computer that he used for email and surfing the net and that Ruby used for some specialized learning programs and games. But a printer? Unless I just hadn't noticed it?

I dialed Brody's number. A strange voice answered.

"Is Brody there," I asked.

"Um, he's just in the bathroom," came the reply.

"Who is this?"

"I'm his nephew, Andrew. Who are you?"

Andrew, Debbie's teenage son. "It's Hilly, your Aunt Gina's friend." A shudder went through me as I pronounced her name. My throat caught.

"Oh hi," Andrew said, "hang on a sec." He shouted, "Uncle Brody, it's Hilly."

I heard Brody's voice replying and then he took the phone.

"Got a visitor, Brody?" I asked.

"Not a visitor. Hold on a sec."

There was a muffled exchange of words and then Brody resumed our conversation. "I just sent Andrew out on an errand. Hilly, what the hell did you tell Debbie about me?"

"Just that you looked awful, unkempt, were lacking sleep, and that you probably weren't eating well."

Brody sighed. "You did a great job of making me sound like a walking, talking sob story. She came in here, guns blazing, and wanted me to pack a bag and move in with her."

"Which you refused to do."

"Of course. She has four kids. I'm not used to all that noise. Gina and Ruby." He paused. "We were a quiet family. Debbie has strong opinions though and I had to negotiate."

"And?"

"Bottom line is her son Andrew has moved in to keep tabs on me and report to his mom. I've been escorted to the barber, I am sure Andrew has a 'to do' list I'm supposed to comply with as he keeps reminding me about things. He's just like his mother."

"Sounds like an organized young man."

"Too organized. A bit OCD if you ask me. Anyhow, I'm being fed regularly and checked up on. Are you happy?"

"Yes," I said. "You needed shaking up. I hate to say it, Brody, but life goes on and you need to remain strong."

"Yeah, Debbie had the nerve to tell me that if Ruby came home and saw me with beard stubble and long hair, I would scare her. I'm sure her kidnappers are a lot scarier. Have you heard anything, Hilly? Is that why you are calling?"

"No news," I said. "But Brody, I was wondering, do you have a printer in the house?"

"No," Brody said. "There's one down in the cottage rental office though. Gina got it when she bought herself a laptop last year. She's converted all our bookkeeping to an online program and ..."

"A laptop?"

"Yeah, why?"

"Brody, you should have told the police she had a laptop. There might be more information on it than there is in that file you gave me. Will you call Lester or do you want me to do it?"

"I didn't think about it, Hilly. Sorry. But it is a good idea. Would you call please? If Andrew hears about this, he'll report it to his mom and she'll be up in arms that I didn't mention it before."

"Okay, I'll call. They'll need you to go and hand it over to them and they may want to search the office in case there's any other information lying around."

"Great. Tell them I'm going back down there now and I'll wait for them. I was there earlier just to check to see if there were any rental requests or messages on the phone."

"I know. I saw you. I was walking the dog."

"About the dog, Hilly – when did you decide to adopt one?"

"I'm just dog sitting for someone," I replied.

"Who," Brody asked.

"Just someone I know," I said

"Hey secrets? We've been friends for years. How come you aren't talking about this?"

"Brody, I'll explain later. I have to call Lester." I hung up.

I called the police station and the receptionist told me Lester was already on the phone. I left a message for him to call me back as soon as possible. He did.

"A laptop?" Lester shouted down the phone line. "Why the heck didn't Brody mention this sooner?"

"He's been in a bit of a fog since Gina died and Ruby disappeared. He said he didn't think about it until I asked him if they had a printer somewhere. Gina used it mainly down at the rental office and that's where the printer is."

"I never asked Brody about a laptop – I just saw the older model he had and asked if Gina ever used it. He said 'no' What made you ask?"

"I just wondered why there were so many printouts in the file when I did not recall ever seeing a printer at Brody's place. He told me about the laptop and printer at the office. He's gone down there and he'll wait for someone to come and get it."

"Great," Lester said. "Hold on a minute."

He put me on hold for a few minutes, then came back to the phone.

"I've sent Harry down there to get it and to talk to Brody. If Gina recorded all her research on it, but didn't print everything out, there could be some good leads there. Good work Hilly. Gotta go. Will call you later."

I had high hopes there would be more clues on the laptop. That and the information the police might get from the stuff Harry had taken from the motel storage unit, including the business card found in the empty purse, might give us some indication of who the people were who had rented the motel cottage and if they were connected to Gina's death. And at last we might be able to identify the body I had found on the beach.

Chapter 13

Brody called me later that afternoon to tell me the police had picked up the laptop and were going to go through Gina's files and her emails.

"I am very confused about all this," he said. "I can't understand why she was looking into this old story and what the connection is to her death."

I didn't want to say that perhaps the killers thought she knew where the gold was buried and had accidentally murdered her when they tried to force her to tell them. I didn't want to give the poor man any more anguish than he was already going through.

"We don't know, Brody. But the police know how to go through this stuff and, if there are any leads, there they will find them and follow up."

"I hope they find something," Brody said. "I miss her so much Hilly and I am so scared for Ruby. Those men, they could do anything to her. She's naive and doesn't always understand what is going on around her. They probably don't know how to deal with her. They may think she's putting them on and … and . . ."

"Hurt her," I finished.

"Yeah," Brody said.

"She didn't look hurt in that photo that was sent to me so let's not go to extremes," I said. Ruby had not looked hurt in the photo, but she did look confused and dazed. Perhaps they were drugging her to keep her quiet. My heart ached for the poor girl. She'd been dealt enough difficulties in life without having to live through seeing her mother killed and then being kidnapped.

"What – oh, Debbie is here with her kids and more food. Hilly, I'm going to gain weight if she keeps feeding me like this."

"She's doing what she knows best, looking after you. Take the pampering and try to get a good night's sleep," I said. "The police are on the case. They are further ahead than they were a couple of days ago. Something's gotta give."

" Hilly, thanks for being there for me."

"No problem," I replied. "That's what friends are for, being there." I hung up and sighed. I didn't wish the situation he was in on anybody.

HD whined and banged her cone against the kitchen table. I guessed it was getting near to supper time and I had to give her another of those pills. Such joy.

What was I going to eat? Right now one of Debbie' comfort food meals would be very welcome. I thought about driving to the point and crashing Brody's dinner, but I knew I would never get out of there what with everyone asking me questions.

It would have to be another microwave dinner. I was going to have to start cooking better meals. But there was just too much going on right now. While I waited for the stogy pasta dish to defrost and cook, I looked down at HD's bowl of kibble which she was enjoying. I wasn't that badly off that I had to eat kibble. Actually my dinner turned out to be halfway decent when washed down with a large glass of chardonnay. Wine always makes meals better.

The next morning, I walked the dog, then hunkered down and got back to working on client requests. The hours flew by and I worked right through lunch. What with traipsing about with Lester and having the dog to look after, I'd fallen behind on my work and had to catch up.

I was just sending off another email to a client when the phone rang. It was Lester.

"Hey Hilly, that laptop lead was a good one. We've found oodles of material on it that Gina did not printout. I'd like to get your thoughts on it. Want to come down and take a look?"

"Sure," I said. "Do I have time for a late lunch – I worked right through since this morning."

"That's fine. Don't want you fainting on us."

"When have I ever fainted, Lester?"

"Well, there was this one time when Carl . . ."

I shuddered. "If you don't mind I'd rather forget that. His prank gave me nightmares for years."

"See ya later," Lester said and hung up.

I let HD out for a pee break while I made a quick sandwich. I'd get a coffee down at the station – after all Lester had said free coffee was part of my perks as a consultant.

He was in one of the conference rooms when I arrived. An officer I didn't recognize was seated in front of the laptop.

"Hilly, Frank, Frank Hilly," Lester said. "Frank is a computer expert from Roxton. We arranged for him to come down and help us out with this. We're also printing out a lot of the material that wasn't in that file Brody gave you."

"Plus going through the emails," Frank added.

"That's where it gets real interesting," Lester said.

"Why?" I poured myself a large cup of coffee from the urn on the credenza while I waited for his answer.

"It appears Gina must have been planning a book on the secret treasure of Paxton Point. We found an outline for the story, all kinds of details we didn't know before and, the icing on the cake is . . ."

"Don't keep me in suspense."

"Gina tracked down Dan's' great granddaughter."

"What," I said spilling my coffee on the conference table.

"She did an online search and found the woman's name, Janet Fredricks. She lives in Bellville," Frank said.

Lester smiled. "And that was the name on that business card I found in the purse at the motel storage unit."

"Have you contacted her?" I asked.

"No," Lester answered, "because calls to her number on the card are only being picked up by an answering service. I've talked to the local police down there and asked them to follow up. Hilly, I have a bad feeling about this."

"You think she's the woman I found on the road?"

"Yeah," Lester said. But not a word to anyone until we get a positive ID okay?"

"Right," I said. "Is there anything on the laptop about this woman?"

"No too much," Franks said, "but they communicated."

"Really?"

"This Janet agreed to meeting Gina just a few days before she was murdered," Frank said.

"Wow. Did they actually meet? Did Gina enter any notes about the interview?"

"It's strange." Lester said, "but Gina was so thorough with all her other research that I'm surprised she didn't include whatever she learned from the granddaughter. But maybe the meeting got called off."

"So far we haven't found anything, but there's still stuff to go through," Frank added.

"That's where you come in," Lester said.

"Me, why?"

"We need another set of eyes on this material. Can you just sit and read and mark anything you think might be of help in this case? You knew Gina well, you knew her style of writing and you can get into her mental state."

"Sure," I said. "But I have to go home and take care of the dog later on."

"That's fine," Lester said. "Just let me know when you want to take a break."

I settled in at the conference table and began to read through the pile of new printouts. I was armed with a stack of stickie notes and a highlighter. A notepad and pen were at hand. Plus more coffee and a chocolate sprinkle doughnut. Lester knew me well.

The first sheet contained an outline of the information she had amassed. Its title was "The Truth about the Treasure of Paxton Point" and contained a list of headings that resembled names of chapters in a book. Each section or chapter had subheads and notes. It really did look as if Gina had been planning to write a book, but why?

I started to read through the sheets of paper. Some of them repeated information I was already familiar with and others contained additional data. Gina had been very thorough in her research. She had been on a lot of websites most normal people wouldn't use for research and I wondered where she had found out about them. If she had shared her project with me I could have helped her, but she didn't for some reason. I felt kind of snubbed, but was curious as to who could have helped.

<u>Wait a minute.</u> There was a new employee at the library. A college graduate no less who had come back to Lamb's Bay to get work experience before moving on to the big city. She would have been up on all the modern search engines.

I walked down the hall to Lester's office, but he wasn't there.

"Gone on a call," the receptionist told me. "Can I help?"

"Do you have the number for the library?"

"Sure." She flipped through some pages and wrote the number on a stickie note. "Just dial 9 to get an outside line."

"Thanks," I said.

I walked back into Lester's office. He was out and I didn't feel like talking about my idea in front of Frank in case I was wrong.

When the call was answered, I asked to speak to Donna Richards, the head librarian.

"Hi Donna, Hilly here."

"Oh hi, Hilly, how can I help you?"

"I was just wondering if Gina had been in the library a lot in the days before, well you know."

"That poor girl," Donna said. "Is there any news on Ruby? That girl loved to come in and look at all the books."

"No news, I'm afraid, but I see by Gina's laptop she was doing some advanced online searches. Did you or that new girl help her out with that?"

"Not me," Donna said. "But hold on and I'll ask Louisa."

A few minutes later, a different voice came down the phone line. "This is Louisa. How can I help you?"

"Hi," I said. "I'm Hilly Barton-Cheswick. I'm consulting with the police department on the death of Gina Paxton."

"Oh," Louisa said in a small voice. "She was such a nice lady."

"Look did she come in there and do a lot of advance searches online?"

"Why, yes," Louisa replied. "She wanted all kinds of material about the so-called treasure of Paxton Point. I've been hearing that story since I was a kid, but never thought it was real. Turns out it really happened."

"Louisa, did she ever say why she was so obsessed with the story?"

"Not really, but the day before she died, she was kind of talking to herself in front of her laptop when I went into one of the study areas. I asked her what she was talking about. She laughed and said, 'oh Louisa I'm just trying to prove or disprove the old story – and publish a book that will put the whole thing to rest for ever.' "

Just then Lester walked into his office and raised an eyebrow when he saw me on his phone.

"Louisa, I'm going to pass you to Captain Spriggs now. Is that okay? I'd like you to tell him what you told me." I handed the phone to Lester.

"Louisa, the new librarian," I whispered.

Lester took the phone and introduced himself. He asked the girl to repeat what she had told me. Lester's eyes widened as he listened.

"Louisa, that's important information. I'm going to send an officer down there to take a statement from you. Okay?"

She must have agreed because Lester left the office, calling for Harry. A couple minutes later, I looked through the window and saw a squad car pulling out of the parking lot.

Lester came back into his office. "What made you call that girl?"

"Just a hunch," I said. "Someone must have been helping Gina with her searches online – she wasn't that computer savvy. I figured it had to be that new girl, the one who just finished her studies – she probably knows all the latest stuff and jumped at a chance to help Gina out with a project. It can't be too exciting for her working in Lamb's Bay."

"I don't know," Lester said. "We've had some excitement with two murders and a kidnapping in the last week. That's enough excitement for me."

"Lamb's Bay can do without that kind of excitement," I said.

"That's for sure," Lester said, nodding.

I went back to the conference room and read through more of the paper printouts which now included the contents of some of Gina's emails. Sid was there as well making notes.

After another hour I looked at the clock. It was time for a break for me and a pee break for HD.

I went down the hall and stuck my head into Lester's office.

"I'm going home to walk the dog and get some supper. Okay? Do you want me to come back this evening?"

"No, that's fine Hilly. I'll call you in the morning if we need more help. Thanks. That lead on the librarian was great."

"Good," I said. "Talk to you tomorrow."

I drove home thinking about food. I decided to stop by the BBQ Grill and get a chicken and trimmings dinner to take out. That would hold me until tomorrow. I really did need to get back to cooking, but somehow I never had the time.

The aroma of the chicken filled the car and my tummy was rumbling by the time I pulled into the driveway. I exited the car, balanced the box of chicken on one hand and fumbled with the other for the new set of keys in my purse. I remembered I needed the green one for the front door. I knew also that it would take time to get used to this new key system and that I had to be patient with myself.

As I walked up the front steps, I could hear HD barking her head off. What the heck? I reached for the front door and found I didn't need my green-coded key. The glass panel in the door had been smashed in which would give an intruder the ability to reach through and unlock my new deadbolt. Oh crap.

HD was still barking but I didn't want to go into the house not knowing who was in there. My gun was no good to me. I'd put it back in my safe when Lester returned it to me.

I ran back to the car with my box of chicken clutched to my chest, got in and locked the doors. Then I called 911.

A few minutes later, Harry and Sid's squad car pulled into my driveway. I rolled the window down and told them about the smashed window panel in the door. Harry took the front and Sid the back. Harry came back a few minutes later.

"Hilly, we need you to call off your dog."

"Why?"

"She's running loose in the yard and she won't let Sid near the house."

"Oh, right." I said.

I stashed my chicken dinner on the passenger seat of the car and went round to the garden gate. Sid was on the other side, held at bay by the frightening sight of HD and her cone. She was in full throttle.

I motioned to Sid to stand aside and went into the garden. HD calmed somewhat when she saw me but was still barking. I got close to her and grabbed her collar, no mean feat with the cone in the way. I pulled off my scarf and slipped it through the collar to form a makeshift leash.

"Go," I said to Sid.

He took off for the back door at a run. I pulled HD through the gate. She was growling and agitated. I got her over to the car and stood there waiting for the policemen to exit the house.

Harry came out shortly and said they had searched everywhere quickly, even in the basement and found no one. "But your office is a mess," he said.

"My office? Oh no." I felt panic rising inside me. I had left Gina's file on the desk instead of putting it back in the safe before I went down to help Lester out at the police station. I wasn't thinking straight when I locked HD in the car.

I followed Harry into the house and went straight to my office. All the items from Gina's research file were gone. My safe hadn't been touched and, when I opened it, my gun was still there. I was relieved. They hadn't stolen my computer or printer, thank goodness. I had insurance, but it takes time to get the replacement money back from those guys.

My shoulders sagged. I had been right. The intruder the other night was looking for Gina's research. Luckily I knew most of the material – and the original clippings and the small notebook – were back at the police station either in a file or on Gina's laptop. I sank into a chair feeling the effects of the adrenaline wearing off. Here I had been looking forward to a glass of wine, a nice dinner, and . . . . <u>Oh no, dinner</u>.

Harry gave me a look that said "what's the problem" as I tore out of my office and went straight to my car. It was too late. The box with my chicken dinner in it was destroyed. Sauce and French fries were all over the upholstery. HD had managed to get free of her cone somehow and had bitten off a huge piece of chicken breast which she was gnawing on.

I knew chicken bones were deadly for dogs. So pulled together every bit of chicken I could find and dumped it into the plastic bag I kept in the car for garbage. I managed to distract HD with the sauce container by holding it under her nose. She stopped worrying at the chicken breast and began to lap up the sauce. However, it sprayed all over the place. I put the chicken breast in the garbage along with the other pieces and then tried to haul the dog out of the car.

HD didn't want to leave the car. She was in love with the chicken and sauce-coated car. I finally managed to wrestle her and her cone out of the front seat and into the driveway. I held on to her with the improvised scarf-leash while I removed soggy French fries from my pants with the other.

I took stock of my situation: A smashed front door, a missing file, a chicken and sauce-covered car and a dog with a cone. Car and dog were in dire need of a bath. Could life get any better?

I heard some chuckling and looked up to see Harry and Sid laughing their heads off.

I saw red. "I just had my house robbed and my dinner stolen and you laugh. What kind of cops are you anyway?"

"Sorry, Hilly," Harry said. She gulped a couple of times and managed to stop giggling. "It was just, well you should have seen it."

"I damn well hope neither of you made a video of that," I said. "If I see it on YouTube, I'm coming after you."

"No ma'am, no YouTube," Harry said. But I noticed Sid was locking his phone in the squad car and somehow I just knew HD, the chicken dinner and I would be entertaining the other cops tonight.

"So what now," I said.

"Well, I'd suggest Dean's car wash," Harry said. "They do a great job of cleaning interiors. My niece puked one day and ...."

"No." I actually stamped my foot. "I mean about the break-in."

"Oh we're investigating," Harry said. "Lester is on his way. I, er, told him to bring you a sandwich since your supper kind of, ah, went to the dog, so to speak."

Sid started giggling again. I shot him my worst "I am pissed off look." It didn't stop him.

You have to excuse Sid," Harry said. "He doesn't have as much experience as I do in appropriate behaviour at crime scenes."

I sighed. "Yeah, well, I guess it was pretty funny. Not the break-in but the dog and the chicken."

HD was leaning against me whining. "Can I go inside the house with the dog?"

"Better to wait until Lester and our crime scene tech gets here," Harry said.

A few minutes later, the tech and Lester showed up. I had several members of the local police department in my front driveway now. I saw a few of my neighbours, usually so quiet and reserved, were gathering at the end of the driveway and chatting to each other. My life was turning into a circus.

"Hilly," Lester said. "Sorry, I thought the locks would help."

"I should have replaced the door, too," I said.

"I was focused on the locks and never thought about that glass panel," Lester admitted.

That's not important now," I said. "Lester, they took Gina's file."

"Damn," Lester said. "Good thing you found out about that laptop and that you gave me the originals of the notebook and the clippings."

"Yeah." HD was pulling on the scarf-leash and pawing at the car door. The smell of BBQ chicken was strong.

"Listen, Lester, I'm going to put the dog in the back yard."

"That's fine," Lester replied.

HD didn't look too happy about being parked in the yard but, hey, I had no choice. I decided I'd go back there and sit with her, but first I wanted to retrieve my purse from the car.

I went back to the driveway. Lester was leaning against the squad car talking on the phone. When he saw me, he hung up and reached into the car.

"Here," he said, handing me a cardboard container.

"What's this?"

"Harry said you needed a sandwich – and I brought you coffee," he said placing a cup on the car roof.

I'd thought the sight of my ruined dinner and my messed-up car would put me off eating, but I was wrong. I was still hungry. I opened the container. "What kind of sandwich?" I asked.

"Harry said it had to be chicken." I rolled my eyes. To Lester's credit he did not laugh. I sighed.

"I'm going to join HD in the garden and keep her quiet," I said. "Can I get her food and water bowl from the kitchen?"

"Fine," Lester said. "It looks as if your intruder didn't go in there."

I went back through the garden gate, balancing my coffee cup and my sandwich. I entered the kitchen through the back door and moved HD's food and water bowls out onto the back porch. The sight of them seemed to calm her down. I sat and listened to her crunch and slurp while I ate my dinner.

Chapter 14

After I ate and the police had finished looking for fingerprints in my office. I was allowed back into the house.

First thing I did was get some warm water and give HD a sponge bath out in the yard. She seemed to think it was some sort of game and I'm not sure which of us got wetter. I was tired out by the time I finished getting the sauce and chicken bits off her coat and dried her with one of my old bath towels. Everyone including me agreed I couldn't stay in the house that night with a broken front door and there was no way I could get it replaced that night. Two break-ins in almost as many days was wearing on my nerves and I was quite relieved when Lester suggested I stay at Brody's for the night.

Harry waited with me until Brody and Andrew came to get us. We climbed into his car: me the dog the cone, her food, my overnight bag and my laptop. We filled the back seat.

Back at the point, I realized that the only spare bed in the house was in Ruby's room. Andrew was sleeping on the pull-out couch in the living room so he could be near to his favorite thing in life – the television.

Brody brought our things into Ruby's room and we faced each other across the small neat bed. "Brody, I didn't think, when Lester suggested I stay here. I mean if you don't want me to use her room?"

"It's fine," Brody said. "You and she were close. She wouldn't mind and, frankly after what's been going on round here, I feel safer that we're all together tonight. You must be freaked out having had two break-ins."

"More like pissed off," I said. "Not only because someone broke in, but because I was stupid enough to leave the copies of Gina's file lying around. Anyhow, at least we have all the originals, the notebook and the printouts down at the station plus other stuff from her laptop."

"What did you find," he asked.

"More information on the robbery back in 1934 and . . ." I paused. Should I tell him about Gina contacting Dan's great granddaughter? I was sure Lester would ask if he knew about it anyway.

"Brody, did Gina ever mention setting up an interview with a woman?"

"An interview? For what?"

I sat down on Ruby's bed. I was suddenly very tired. I looked up at Brody.

"Gina tracked down Dan's great granddaughter and arranged to meet her to interview her about the family history, what she knew about the robbery and the murder of Elmont. But there are no notes on the laptop about that so we don't know if they did meet."

"Do we know her name?"

"Lester is keeping it confidential right now as the police are trying to contact her. I just thought Gina might have gone away for a day without saying where she was going or told you she was going to meet someone."

Brody looked thoughtful. "Gina's agenda is with the police. If she made an appointment, it would be in there. She was very meticulous about keeping that book up to date."

"Right," I said. "I'll call Lester in the morning and tell him to have someone go over it." I yawned. Right now I'm bushed. I know it is kind of early but I really need some sleep. I didn't get any last night."

"So turn in. Do you want anything? Coffee? Hot chocolate?"

"Oh, no more of anything, Brody. I need to sleep. Where's HD?"

"Andrew has her watching TV with him. You want her in here tonight?"

I shook my head. "She can sleep out there with him if she wants. Though she usually sleeps with me."

"So where does this dog come from again?" Brody asked. "You promised me a story."

"She belongs to Zach," I said

"Zach, the creep who cheated on you? Hilly you haven't seen him in a long time – or have you?

"No, I haven't, but he called out of the blue and asked me to look after her while he is in hospital having surgery. He said he might have cancer."

"Too bad for him, but he deserves it," Brody said. "But couldn't his fabulous girlfriend or his sister look after the animal? Or even send it to a kennel?"

"I know," I said. "I'm a sucker. The girlfriend left him two years ago, his sister is allergic to dogs and he didn't want the animal pining away in a kennel since he didn't know how long he would be in hospital."

"So you were the solution. How convenient. You're not going to see him again are you?

"No way," I said. "I was stupid to agree to look after the dog, though I must say I enjoy her company and she has earned her keep attacking the intruder the other night. I feel bad that she got wounded. But once I hear Zach is back home, I'm going to drop her off in Roxton at his place and change my phone number."

"Good girl," Brody said. "And I'll ride shotgun to make sure he understands he is not wanted in your life."

"Fine. Now you know all about the dog. Can I go to sleep?"

"Sure," he said. "I put some towels on that chair for you."

"Great. Thanks for this, Brody."

"No problem," he said and left, closing the door behind him.

I was ready to pass out in my clothes, but forced myself to stay awake while I changed into my pyjamas, brushed my teeth and then fell into bed. HD might come looking for me in the night, but there was no room for her in that little single bed. She must have realized that because when I got up in the morning she was curled up beside Andrew in the pull-out couch.

It was the smell of coffee that had woken me. Nice dark, percolated coffee. Gets me every time. "Morning, Brody," I said.

"Morning." He handed me a big mug of the delicious brew. "Sleep okay?"

I nodded as I sipped. "Thanks for taking us in."

HD got out of bed in the living room, padded into the kitchen and whined at us.

"Toilet time," I said.

We let her out into the small fenced yard and perched ourselves on the bench of the picnic table.

It was a perfect Lamb's Bay day. The sky was blue, the gulls were circling, the sun was illuminating every inch of the craggy point. The smell of the sea at low tide hung in the air. I breathed it in – there is no other smell like that. It spoke of seaweed and salt, marine creatures and the damp sand of a seashore morning.

"Gina always loved this time of day," Brody said. "Sitting here watching the sea and the gulls. Sipping hot coffee. Talking. Some of the best moments in our marriage. Sounds strange I know, but we always felt so close at those times. Something about the point and its beauty bound us together."

I could see tears in his eyes as he wandered off to help HD who'd gotten her cone caught on a plant stake.

I went over to join him. "We've got more information now than we did before. Lester has lots of people working on this. They even brought in a computer specialist from Roxton to work on Gina's computer. It won't bring Gina back, I know, but if it will help us find Ruby. . ."

He nodded and remained silent

"You have to stay strong for her, Brody. When she comes back, she will need you more than ever without her mother here."

"You mean, if she comes home," Brody said softly.

"Be positive," I replied.

"I'm trying," he said, "but it's hard.

Later that morning, I left HD with Andrew while Brody drove me out to my house. I had arranged for Dean's Auto to come and pick up my car for cleaning. They arrived shortly after and took the car away. I checked inside the car to make sure I'd left nothing of importance in there and it still smelled like chicken and sauce. I hoped they could get the smell out. I loved BBQ chicken but didn't want to have to smell it every time I drove my car.

Brody cleared up the broken glass from the door panel for me. The repairman turned up to install a new door and, just as he finished, Mr. Jenkins was back.

"You can't blame this break-in on the locks I installed," he said. "My lock did its job. It was the door that was at fault."

"Yes, I agree," I said. "A faulty door. Please just install a new lock on the new door so I can move back home."

He got to work and I walked away. The door was at fault. Honestly. The break-in was the fault of the burglar, not the door, nor the locks. When Mr. Jenkins was finished and had handed over yet another new key, purple-tipped this time, I paid him and he left. Brody and I headed back to the point so I could pick up HD and my things.

I offered to pay for takeout burgers to share with Andrew, but Brody said they had enough casseroles in the refrigerator to feed an army and that I had to come and help them eat some of them.

The three of us were enjoying Debbie' famous tuna, green bean, macaroni and cheese casserole when Brody looked out the window and announced, "We're getting company."

Andrew and I looked out and saw a squad car making its way up the point road.

"Cool, cops, "Andrew said.

"Just the dog for a walk, please," Brody said, handing him the leash. He and I stepped outside to meet the car. It was Lester.

"Got some news," he said. "Mind if I come in?"

"No problem," Brody said.

Andrew had taken off with HD for a ramble in the direction of the lighthouse so we were dog-free for the time being.

"Want coffee?" Brody asked. "There's more macaroni and cheese casserole if you're hungry."

"No, I'm fine. Can we sit at the table?"

"Sure."

"Brody, I want you to think hard. Does the name Janet Fredericks mean anything to you? Did Gina ever mention that name?"

Brody took a minute to answer, then shook his head. "No. I don't remember her ever talking about someone named Janet. Why?"

Lester pulled two photos out of an envelope. One was the dead woman I had found on the shore road. The other was the same woman, but when she was alive.

"She was the body on the shore road?" I asked

"We got positive identification this morning. The police in Bellville checked out the lead for us. The woman disappeared a few days ago and her fingerprints match."

"Her fingerprints were on file?"

"She had a job at a high-tech firm. They did security checks on all their employees. The Bellville police got us access and they match the ones from the dead woman. That's her. Dan's' great granddaughter."

We stared silently at the photo.

She looks, what, 30s," I asked.

"35," Lester said. "And something else interesting."

"What?"

"She's a certified diver."

"The equipment in the SUV the motel owner told us about," I
blurted.

"Yeah and this morning Ms. Unger confirmed this was the
woman who rented the cottage from her."

"Ms. Unger? Who's she? Cottage? What diving equipment? I
never heard any of this." Brody jumped up and started to
pace.

"Calm down, Brody," Lester said. "Sit down and I'll fill you
in. Actually perhaps we do need some coffee."

As we waited for the percolator to do its job, Lester told Brody
about the Fair Haven Motel and Cottages and all about the
people who had stayed there. He explained about finding the
business card in the purse and how that led to identifying the
dead woman. I could see Brody was overwhelmed by all this
new information. But I remembered his comment last night
about Gina's agenda.

"Lester," I said. "Brody mentioned last night that Gina kept an
agenda which your staff took when they were investigating
her death. There could be some information about this
supposed meeting in there."

"I'll have my guys pull out it of the evidence locker. Thanks."
The coffee was ready so the three of us sat sipping while
Brody asked Lester all kinds of questions. Lester fielded them
diplomatically and I noticed he left out some of the details that
only those of us working on the case would know.

Just then HD and Andrew came back from their walk. I asked
Lester if he could drive me and the dog back to my place. I
wanted to save Brody a trip and it would give me a chance to
talk to Lester privately.

We took off in the squad car with HD and her cone occupying
the back seat along with our luggage –my overnight bag and a
larger bag with dog "stuff" in it.

"You sure you want to go back home," Lester asked.

"Where else would I go? Lester, I had to sleep in Ruby's bed last night. Think of how weird that was for Brody and for me. No, I'm better off at home. The burglar got Gina's file so I don't think there will be any other break-ins. Besides, I had a solid door installed and a new lock from Mr. Jenkins."

"Great," Lester said. "Alarm system?"

"No way," I replied. I'm still not a fan."

"Well you may want to think about it. When Zach gets better, HD goes home and there won't be a canine advance warning system on the premises anymore."

Lester had a good point and he knew it. "I know, I know. Okay I'll think about it."

"Good girl," Lester said.

"Gee, thanks."

"Snippy today aren't we?" He smiled "Think Brody's going to be okay?"

"I don't know Lester, I don't know. What I do know is that he'd be a whole lot better if we found Ruby."

"We're working on it. What I didn't tell Brody was that Janet had a cousin named Ralph Benson who was also a diver."

"What, really?"

"He's not around either. So I think whatever Janet was up to that he was in on it."

"Perhaps he's the one who killed Gina and took Ruby," I said.

"Maybe Janet didn't agree with it. She must be the one who dropped off that envelope at my place."

"Right again. Her fingerprints were on it."

"So the 'he' that she warned me about in the message must be her cousin. It gives us another lead."

Lester pulled into my driveway and I unloaded HD and kept a tight hold on her leash as I retrieved our gear from the backseat of Lester's car. "Thanks for the ride," I told Lester.

"You're welcome, Hilly," he said. "Stay safe."

As he drove away from the house, for the first time in years I was nervous being alone out here at my home. It was kind of isolated surrounded by all those trees. It also looked different with the new front door. Before, the glass panel in the front door had always given the house a friendly appearance. Now with the solid door, it appeared to be frowning at the world. Shadows passed over the sun and a cool wind came up. There would be rain soon. Pity since the day had started out so fair. I tugged on HD's leash. "Come on girl. Let's go home."

Chapter 15

I tried settling down after we got back into the house. Lester had said I could tidy up in my office, so I went in there to work on that. My heart wasn't in it. I am not the tidiest of persons at any time, but my disorder has order to it. The burglar had completely disturbed the balance of my office and its contents.

HD seemed happy to be back in her bed in the kitchen. She didn't need any more walking after her ramble with Andrew, so I had no excuse not to get to work. But I procrastinated. I put on a load of laundry – a small one. I put all errant dishes in the dishwasher. I checked and rechecked all the windows and doors to make sure they were closed and locked.

Finally I gave myself a good talking to about these delaying behaviours and strode into my office, a coffee in one hand and my purse in the other.

I started with my desk. All my office supplies – stapler, tape dispenser and extra rolls of tape, pens, pencils, paperclips, notebook, etc. – had been emptied from the drawers and thrown all over the place. I couldn't figure out why since Gina's file had been sitting right in the middle of my desk, easy to find. Perhaps he or she thought I had other information stashed away somewhere – with my paperclips? Seriously?

All files had been pulled out of my four-drawer filing cabinet and emptied onto the floor. Hoo boy that was going to take a while to sort out and refile. I could count myself lucky that my safe and computers – laptop and desktop -- had not been stolen. But wait a minute, had they tried to access my computer files?

I hit the on button and the computer started. The sign-in screen came on with a message that the wrong password had been used, try again. So he had tried to get into the computer. My password was an unusual one, a combination of two halves of words in two different languages – Latin and Greek – thanks to my father and his fascination with the classics. It also included a random series of numbers that had no relationship to anything in my life. That made it harder to try and figure out. Perhaps that explained the excessive mess in my office. Frustrated by my computer, the intruder had done a number on my files and office supplies.

My laptop had been with me in my car's trunk and I guess he was in too much of a hurry to try and disconnect the desktop and haul it away. It was an older model so a tad heavier than the latest models, but still fully functional and served my purposes for now. I'd have to upgrade in the coming months though.

For the next couple of hours, I picked up and sorted. By the time the phone rang in the late afternoon, my back was killing me and I'd given in to my anger at my office being violated. I was mumbling curse words under my breath as I worked.

"Barton-Cheswick," I said.

"Hi, Hilly, it's me."

"Me, who?" I asked, juggling the phone and a stack of papers.

"Tracy."

"Oh, hi, Tracy. Give me a minute." I put the papers on the only clear section of my desk and lowered my aching back and the rest of me into my comfy office chair. "What's up?"

"I just thought I'd check in with you; let you know how Zach is."

"Okay."

Tracy cleared hr throat. "He's, well . . ." Her voice trailed off. Uh oh, bad news. "Tracy, spit it out."

"It's just that he will be going home in a couple of days, so if you are too busy to go to the hospital, you'll be able to visit him there. I'll let you know when he is home. But . . ."

There's always a but. "But," I repeated.

"He won't be able to look after HD right away so is it okay if she stays like another week, or two?"

"Week or two?"

"Yeah, he can't walk her right now and since he lives in an apartment, it would be difficult. Can you keep her, as a favor to Zach?"

A favour for Zach. I began to feel a slow burn of anger. "I don't do favors for Zach," I said. "But I'll do this for HD. She's been through enough and, besides she has to go to the vet up here in a few days anyway."

"Vet?" Tracy asked. "Why is she seeing a vet up there? She has her own vet down here. What's wrong?"

There was no way I could sugar-coat this. "She got shot, Tracy."

"What?" Tracy screamed so loudly it sounded as if she was standing right beside me. "What? Is she okay?"

"She's fine," I said. "The bullet grazed her ear and she's got a couple of stitches. She's taking antibiotics and has to wear a plastic cone so she doesn't interfere with the wound. Other than that everything is going well."

"Going well? You shot the dog? What, were you playing around with that stupid gun of yours or something? Did you take her to a shooting range and she got in the way?"

"Tracy, number one guns aren't stupid, just some of the people who use them and I'm not stupid. Number two, I didn't shoot her, the burglar did."

"You had a break-in? Oh my god," Tracy said in a calmer voice.

"Tracy, everything is under control and since she is wearing that cone and needs to see the vet, she can stay a few more days."

Tracy was still fixated on the idea of HD getting shot and was blaming me. "You know I hate them. Guns, I mean. Perhaps you should lock yours away until HD comes back to Roxton. Honestly, how could you let her get shot? What am I going to tell Zach? He'll be devastated."

"Tracy, you aren't paying attention. I didn't let her get shot; she chased the burglar out of the house. He fired a shot and nicked her ear. End of story."

"Oh, so she's a hero. How wonderful. She protected you. Dogs only protect people they like."

Her remark conjured up the perverse image of a dog refusing to save someone on the grounds that "I never liked him." Oh boy, Tracy was odd at times. These writers.

Tracy continued babbling. "Zach will be so pleased to hear about it – well not about her getting shot, but about the fact she likes you so much."

"Yeah, that's strange enough as it is. She took to me right away and doesn't seem to be missing Zach."

"She's had a tough time being ignored a lot this past year and a half."

"Ignored? For a year and a half?"

"In the beginning, Zach and HD went everywhere together. Even to the office. But then Zach got this big contract from one of his corporate customers. Their headquarters is located in Europe so he's had to travel at times. You know how he is about chasing the almighty dollar. So HD has been spending a lot of time at the kennel and . . ."

"Hold on," I said. "You mean she's used to going to the kennel?"

"Yes, but she does mope when she's in there. She's gotten used to the staff and everything but doesn't look herself when she comes home. It's one of the best in Roxton, but dogs miss having their owners around. However, when Zach is home, he's too busy to spend much time with her. He even has a dog walker for her because he doesn't have time to go out with her. That's why I was so glad that she was going to be spending time with you."

"I thought she hated the kennel and that's why I needed to look after her."

"Oh Hilly," Tracy said. "I guess some wires got crossed between you and Zach. He must have said something you misunderstood and that's why you volunteered to have her for a while. Which I think is great, also the fact that you and Zach are communicating more often. He's changed Hilly. Give him a chance."

"Er, Tracy, Zach and I do not communicate at all," I replied gritting my teeth.

"Not well, I agree," Tracy said. "I'm sorry if you feel you volunteered because of a mistake."

"Tracy, I did not volunteer."

"But Zach said . . ."

I cut her off. "We are both aware of what Zach is capable of saying when he wants his own way. Damn it, I'm mad I fell for his act."

"What act?" Tracy asked cautiously.

I took a deep breath to calm myself then launched into my story. "He called me out of the blue, said he was in hospital, that they thought he had cancer. He said because of your allergies you couldn't take HD and she hated the kennel though he had been forced to use it a couple of times. She always lost weight when she was there due to pining. Would I do him the big favor of taking her and, if he was going to die, would I either keep her or find her a good home."

There was dead silence. I thought I'd crossed a line and Tracy had hung up. But she was still there.

"That rotten bastard," she said. "He told me you'd been talking together lately and that when he said he needed an operation, you offered to look after the dog."

"Tracy, I didn't even know HD existed until he called a few days ago. If he doesn't have cancer, I'm liable to shoot him."

Tracy said quietly, "that was a lie. He doesn't have cancer. He had a hernia operation."

My anger spilled over. "That rotten son of a SOB," I shouted. "He lied and used that as an excuse to contact me. I haven't spoken to him since I left him. I didn't even know he wasn't with Cindy anymore."

"My brother is a total jerk," Tracy said. "You don't have to shoot him, Hilly. I may do that for you. I'm so sorry he stuck you with HD. I guess the plan was to use her to get you emotionally involved, then he could worm his way into your life."

"Fat chance. What a cheap trick using such a lovely animal to try and get your ex back."

"I agree," Tracy said, "but . . ."

"But, what?"

"It's a great plot twist. May I use it in one of my upcoming novels?"

These romance writers. "Sure be my guest and make sure the jerk's name is Zach."

"You sure you want that?" she asked. "In my books, the lovers always reconcile. My fans would expect no less. But I understand that isn't going to be the case with Zach and you. Look, are you sure you don't want me to come and get the dog? She can go back to the kennel and they'll get their vet to take care of her stitches."

"That's kind of you," I said, "but you can't be around her. You don't need dog hair and dander on the car's upholstery or you'll be the next one in the hospital."

Talking about dog hair on the upholstery reminded me to call Dean's and find out when my cleaned car would be ready.

"I would have to find someone else to drive her back here, that's for sure," Tracy said. "I can't think of any other way to help you."

"It's okay. She can stay," I replied. "She's been traumatized so let her be for now. But once that conniving brother of yours is home and HD is better, we'll arrange to get her back to him without me or you being involved. And the one thing you can do for me, Tracy, is to tell him not to contact me ever again or try to come near me. I'll get a restraining order."

"You got it," Tracy said.

"Just don't tell him I'd like to shoot him or he'll say I'm threatening him and go to the police."

"That would be just like him to make out he's the victim. It wasn't easy growing up with him," Tracy said. "I could tell you stories. One day, over a nice bottle of wine. I'll come down and visit when HD is back with Zach."

"That's an idea," I said.

"Do you need any extra food, etc., for her? And let me know what the vet bill is. I'll make sure he gives me the money and I'll reimburse you."

"Thanks, Tracy. There is one question you could answer for me."

"What's that?"

"Why the hell does the poor animal have a name like HD? What was Zach thinking? Most people call their pets something like Fluffy or Spot. Even a person's name like Harold would be more appropriate."

"She's a girl," Tracy said. "Harold would not be appropriate. And because of Zach's lies I thought you knew what HD stood for."

"No. Enlighten me."

"Hilly Dog."

"What?"

"Hilly Dog. He named her Hilly after you."

"He named his dog after me. What the hell for?"

"Because, after Cindy left and he didn't meet anyone else, he said he missed you so much. He realized that he'd made a mistake in leaving you for her."

"The ass said he left me? Sorry, I kicked him out because he was cheating."

"Oh, "Tracy said in a small voice. "Sorry about that too, but remember, I've only ever heard his side of things."

"When you come down to visit, I'll tell you mine. Right now I'm just too angry. But I will tell you this. One day, Zach said he had a meeting and left the office. I went home early because I wasn't feeling well. I walked in and found the two of them naked on my living room sofa."

"Ouch," Tracy said. "Zach really is a bastard."

"And he had the nerve to name his dog after me? He's sick. Really sick."

"Hilly, I don't know what to say or do."

"Me neither, Tracy."

The line between us fell quiet. Then a series of barks broke the silence.

"Is that HD?" Tracy asked.

"In full throttle. Someone must be outside."

"You'd better go. Call 911 if it is that burglar again."

"Of course, but I'm looking out the window and it's a police car. Probably Lester or one of his men."

"Lester? New man in your life, Hilly?"

"No, old friend and police chief. I'm going to hang up. Take care."

"Okay. Rest assured that my brother will be getting a piece of my mind when I see him. I am so glad we talked. I'll never trust him again."

"Me neither," I said. "Go get him, Tracy. But don't shoot him."

"Can't even aim a gun," she said. "Hugs."

I ran to the front door and yanked it open to find Lester on the doorstep. HD recognized him and stopped barking. He patted her. "Got some news."

"What news? Why didn't you call?"

"You were on the land line and your cell was off."

Damn, I forgot to take my charger to Brody's and the battery must have run out. "What's up?"

"The cops down in Belleville have located the address of Janet's brother and are planning to raid the place in the next hour. We think he might be holding Ruby there."

"Oh my god," I said, dragging HD back into the house.

"I knew your car was still being cleaned so I came to take you down to the station. Brody is on his way there now. If they find Ruby, we'll go straight down there. We'll wait for news at the police station."

I wrestled HD into the kitchen and replenished her food bowls. Then I grabbed my purse and followed Lester out to the car after making sure I locked the door.

Before we pulled out of the driveway Lester said, "Hilly, do you have a gun in there?" He pointed to my hobo-style purse. "Looks big enough."

"No, should I?"

"No. Please leave any shooting to the professionals."

"Who said I was going to shoot anyone?"

Lester kept his eyes on the road as he drove. "If we find Ruby, and they've hurt her in any way, I wouldn't put it past you to give in to your emotions."

"Just because I'm a woman? That's discriminatory." I was surprised Lester would say such a thing.

Lester looked offended. "No, not just because you are a woman. I'd say the same thing to Brody if he was sitting in that seat. I'd feel like both of you do. You know I have a girl about the same age. In this situation, I'd have to step aside and leave my gun at home because I know what I'd be liable to do. People like us, we care too much."

"Too much? How can one care so much that it would drive them to shoot someone? I would think their focus would be on getting their loved one back."

"I've seen it happen," Lester said as he drove us back to the station. "I want you and Brody safely at the station while this is going on, so I can make sure of neither of you do something stupid out of love for Ruby and mess things up. Got it?"

I stared at him. I saw his point, but I wasn't happy about being kept out of the action.

Lester sensed what I was feeling. "Look, Brody is really the person I am most concerned about. I need you to help me keep him stable until we know the outcome of the raid. Your other role if, and that's a big if, Ruby is found will be to provide support for both of them. They are going to need it. Are you with me on this?"

"Yeah, Lester, I get it. I'll behave. And keep Brody out of trouble as much as I can."

Privately, I vowed that if Ruby had been harmed in any way, even a broken fingernail, I would go out of my way to do something to her kidnapper and, since Lester didn't want me shooting him, then I'd try for a well-aimed kick where it would hurt the most.

Chapter 16

Brody beat us to the station and was pacing up and down in Lester's office.

"Sorry, Lester," the receptionist said. "I told him to wait in the conference room but he barged into your office and demanded to know where you were. I told him you'd gone to get Hilly since she doesn't have a car right now. Sorry to hear about the mess in your car, Hilly."

Great. I bet Harry and Sid had entertained the whole staff with that video of HD and I along with the chicken, the sauce and particularly the shot of me wiping French fries off my clothes while trying to control a sauce-crazed dog..

Lester had gone ahead into his office to talk to Brody. I heard raised voices.

"We need to be there," Brody shouted. "Why are you telling me to stay here? I want to be there when they find my daughter. Right, Hilly?" He shot a furious look in my direction as I stepped into the office.

"Let's take this into the conference room," Lester said. "We're disturbing the staff."

We followed him down the hall to the conference room at the back of the building. Huh I thought. Disturb the staff? They were probably drawing lots as to who would eavesdrop on this conversation. It wasn't often that someone raised their voice to Lester and I don't think any of us who knew Brody well had ever seen him angry like this.

Lester shut the door behind us. "Now Brody, I want you to listen and I told Hilly the same thing. We have no idea if Ruby is even there. They could have all left; the cops in Belleville might have bad information. Who knows? I just want the two of you here where I can give you the latest information."

"And keep an eye on us," Brody shouted. "I know you Lester. You like to be in control of the situation. I want to leave." He walked towards the door, but Lester put out his hand and stopped him

"Brody," he said. His tone made Brody pause. It was Lester's warning tone. It said: "Don't listen to me and all hell will break loose."

Brody backed down and went to sit at the table. I was already sitting, keeping out of the way. There were tears in Brody's eyes.

"Hilly, what do you think?" Brody asked. "You're my friend. You're Ruby's godmother."

"Brody," I said, taking his hand in mine. "We have to be patient. What Lester says is true. We don't even know if Ruby is there. And if she is, you might do something that puts her in jeopardy."

"How could I put my own child in jeopardy? Don't you think she's in enough danger?"

"I agree. But what if you got angry and, well, tried to go after the man holding her prisoner. He might over-react and bullets could fly. Someone could get hurt. How do you think Ruby would feel if she saw her father shot? She's already probably seen her mother murdered."

Okay, that was hard to say and Brody looked shocked. But I had to get through to him, otherwise he might take off. We didn't need a loose cannon heading for Belleville.

Brody sighed and nodded. "I understand, but I wouldn't do that. I mean, why would I?"

"We care too much," I said. Lester nodded at me Hi eyes said "keep going."

"Normally, we wouldn't even know what was going on down in Belleville until it was all over," I said. "Lester has let us in on this information because he's a friend and he knows we both want to know the outcome of the police raid as soon as possible."

"That's right," Lester said. "And, if Ruby is there, I'll make sure both of you get to Belleville as fast as possible."

"It's a three-hour drive," Brody said. "We could start for Bellville and if we aren't needed, we could turn around and come back. Lester, I won't be able to wait that long to see my child."

"You won't have to," Lester said. "We'll get you there by helicopter a lot faster. Got it all arranged and standing by. We can have you there as soon as possible. If Ruby is there. Now, I have to leave you folks and go do my job. As soon as I have any news, trust me, I'll let you know."

Lester left shutting the door behind him.

I could feel Brody's stress radiating from him. I patted his hand. I really didn't know what else to say or do.

"Thanks for being here, Hilly," Brody said. "You were always a good friend. Ruby loves you."

"And I love her," I replied. "Probably not as much as you because you're her father, but as much as if she was my own daughter. I want her home as much as you do."

We sat there quietly for about half an hour. There was a knock at the door and we both shot to our feet.

The door opened and we saw the receptionist holding a tray on which there were two mugs, a pot of coffee and a plate of sandwiches. "Lester said to bring in food and drink," she said.

"Is there any news?" Brody asked.

She shook her head. "It will probably be a while yet. Lester will come see you as soon as he can."

I asked Brody if he wanted any coffee. He nodded. The receptionist smiled at me and left. I put a cup of coffee in front of him – milk and two sugars, just the way I knew he liked it. I placed a napkin beside the cup with an egg salad sandwich on it.

"Not hungry," he said, sipping the coffee.

"When did you last eat?"

"Lunchtime. But I'm not hungry." He pushed the sandwich and napkin away.

"Well, I know I could do with a sandwich." I helped myself to an egg salad sandwich and a sliced ham one. They were good. I sipped my coffee. It was something to do while we waited. I noticed Brody ate his sandwich finally and I was pleased. We both needed to keep up our strength for whatever lay ahead of us.

Two hours passed. Brody was dozing and I was trying to finish a crossword puzzle I'd found in a magazine on one of the shelves in the room. Suddenly the door flew open and Lester walked in. He shut the door behind him, sat down and set his coffee cup in front of him.

"Lester?" Brody said, raising his voice slightly. I was holding my breath.

"She wasn't there," Lester said. I let my breath out. Brody lowered his head into his hands.

"What happened?" I asked

"They went in, but Ralph Benson wasn't there. They found a room where someone had been held; there was a girl's t-shirt in the room. You recognize this, Brody?" He put a photo in front of Brody who raised his head and grabbed the photo.

"It's hers," he whispered. And covered his face with his hands, dropping the photo back on the table.

"Okay, that's a start," Lester said.

"Was there, is there, I mean . . .? Brody mumbled from between his hands.

"No sign of a body or blood," Lester said. I winced. Couldn't he have put that in a little bit nicer way? "But . . ."

"But what?" I blurted. "Don't keep us in suspense, Lester."

"They found the third member of the gang. A man named Carl Withers." He placed another photo in front of both of us. "Either of you seen this guy before?"

We both looked at the photo and then shook our heads.

"Harry drove over to Fair Haven to the Unger's and just called to say that Daisy woman confirmed he was the third man renting her cottage. "

"He was the only one the Belleville police found?"

"Yeah," Lester said. "Actually, he wasn't in the house, He was in the nearby field. Looks like Ralph decided to eliminate him before he left. He'd been shot. He managed to get away from the house but passed out from shock in the field. Police found him by following the blood trail and got him to hospital. He's going to make it. Let's hope he can tell us something when he comes around."

"When he comes around?" Brody asked. "I thought you said he was okay."

"Let me clarify, he's okay but in need of surgery," Lester said. "The Belleville police will interview him as soon as the doctors allow it. Meanwhile, there's no other news. We've got an alert out for Ralph and Ruby. His place was set back from the road, but his nearest neighbors were interviewed. They said he always drove a late model tan sedan but that recently, they had noticed a dark blue SUV going in and out of the driveway. It's not there now so we presume he's driving it and," he paused, "that he has Ruby with him."

'Ruby,' Brody said, jumping to his feet. "Oh my god, what if some stupid cop tries to pull them over and there's a situation and this Ralph shoots her and . . .," Brody was flipping out. I went over and put my arms round his shoulders. He tried to shake me off but I held on tight.

"Shh, Brody. Calm down. That's not going to happen, right Lester?" I glared at him.

"Instructions are for any officer who sees them to call for backup first and only then to approach with caution. We all want to avoid a situation like the one you have playing out in your head right now."

"I feel so helpless," Brody said. I let go of him and he slumped into his seat.

"I know, Brody, I know," I said. "We both do. But we have to be patient."

"I'm not good at that," he said. "Not at all."

"It's going to be some time before the police get to interview this Carl. Why don't you go home, get some rest? As soon as I hear something I will let you know."

"Brody, you okay with that?" I asked.

"I want to stay here," he said. "But you can leave if you want."

"Brody, I have to be honest with you," Lester said. "It could be we only get news tomorrow morning. And, by the way, don't you have your nephew Andrew staying with you? Perhaps you should go check on him."

"He's a big boy," Brody said.

I wanted to stamp my foot. When Brody Paxton was stubborn, it was like trying to move a block of cement to get him to listen and change his mind. "You are being so stubborn, Brody Paxton," I said. "And if you are worn out when Ruby is found, you won't be much use to her. She'll need her father more than ever now."

"Gee, thanks for reminding me, Hilly," Brody said wryly. "As if I didn't know that."

"Whoa there, I was just trying to keep your spirits up and be supportive. No need to take that tone." I was tired and feeling huffy.

"Hilly, Brody," Lester said, "we're all worn out and we need to take a step back instead of butting heads."

I took a deep breath. "Look, Brody, I'm sorry," I said.

Brody gave me a weak smile. "Me too It's just that . . ."

"I know. Do you want me to come out to the point and stay there tonight? That is if you don't mind having the dog around? I'm concerned about you being on your own."

"I won't be alone, Andrew is there." He turned to Lester. "All right, I'll go home and I promise not to do anything stupid like try to go down to Belleville."

"Wouldn't do you any good if you did," Lester said. "Carl will be sedated and under police guard."

"And I suppose you gave them my description so I couldn't try anything, like perhaps saying I was next of kin and I needed to see him?" Brody asked.

"Yeah, we covered that one," Lester replied. "I faxed them a photo. I think I know you a bit too well, Brody."

Brody gave a half smile. "I promise to be good, okay? But Lester, this is killing me."

"It is killing all of us, Brody," I said.

Brody nodded and put his jacket. I followed him down the hall to the front of the building and out the front door. "You okay driving," I asked.

"Hilly, all I've had is two coffees and an egg salad sandwich, not booze. You can call Andrew to check on me and, if it makes you feel any better, I'll call you as soon as I get home."

"Then do me a favour and stay there," Lester said." If I call to check and you aren't there, you're the next one I put out an alert on."

"Yeah," Brody said. "I hear you." He walked over to his car, got in and drove out of the parking lot in the direction of the point.

"Thank goodness we got him to go home," I said.

"Let's wait until I hear from Andrew," Lester replied.

"Andrew?"

"I told him to text me to confirm his uncle came home. And to keep me posted if he goes out anywhere. Meanwhile, let's get you over to Dean's."

"Dean's?"

"Your car is ready. I got them to stay open a bit longer so you could pick up your car."

"Great," I said. "But I don't need a drive, Lester. It's only three blocks from here and frankly after the stressful time we've had, I could do with a short walk in the fresh air."

"Okay Hilly. Take it easy tonight. Chill with the pooch – and her cone." He chuckled as he headed for the front door of the building.

I called after him, "I hope you get some news."

He turned and nodded. "Let's hope Carl is able to tell us something that will help us to locate Ruby – and catch Ralph." Just then Lester's cell rang. I looked at him questioningly. "Maureen," he said. "Bye Hilly." He went inside and I turned to walk to Dean's Auto Shop and Car Wash.

I walked the three blocks to the car wash slowly, savoring the fresh air after the hours spent in the conference room. As I walked, I thought about the case and how complicated things were getting.

Lamb's Bay had always been a pretty quiet seaside town. Crimes happened, as they did in many communities, but they were usually small potatoes compared to this case. Two murders, one gang member shot, a girl kidnapped. It was the stuff of a television series or a movie-of-the-week. I hoped the case would be solved soon, with Ruby back home safe and sound plus Gina's and Janet's killer caught. But right now we had no idea where Ruby and Ralph were, nor if Ruby was safe. Unless Lester was holding out on us and I didn't think he was.

At the car wash, I was presented with a hefty bill for detailing the car inside and out. No residue from my unfortunate dinner remained when I inspected the interior. The car smelled of cleaning products, not BBQ sauce. The paintwork shone, the windows sparkled and the upholstery looked as good as new.

I paid the bill with my credit card reflecting that between the vet bill and this one, my budget was taking a real hit this month. Oh well, It was almost the end of the month.

I'd have to knuckle down and do some billing in the morning so I could get some more cash flowing in. In the meantime, I sincerely hoped there wouldn't be any other big bills turning up.

As I drove home, I tried to get my mind off worrying about the case. I put the radio on but not one channel was playing any kind of music I wanted to listen to so I put it off. I focused on driving and worked at banishing all other thoughts until I got home.

Unfortunately, temporarily blocking the case data from my brain left room for remembering all about the conversation I'd had with Tracy earlier in the day.

By now Tracy would have spoken to Zach and told him we were on to his scam. What a creep he had become. Who was I kidding? He'd always had that side to him, but I just didn't see it – I was too much in love and forgave too much. I'd never do that again.

That poor dog. Zach had a nerve using her for his schemes. She was a sweet animal, very protection-conscious, a talent I definitely appreciated. Without her warning, that intruder could have come upstairs in the night and murdered me as well. The thought made me shiver. Lester was right. I should get an electronic alarm system. Or a dog. Both could be pricey, but only one could curl up with you at night and give you companionship.

I knew I would miss HD when she had to go back to Zach. HD, what dumb name for a dog. I refused to call her that anymore. But she was used to it. What could I do? And then it came to me – HD sounded like Heidi. We'd try that.

I was so pleased with my idea that I overshot my own driveway and had to turn around in my neighbor's one. She peered out the window and frowned at me. I'm probably notorious now, I thought, what with all the cop cars they've seen at my house.

A couple of hours later, as I returned from a walk with the dog and had just sat down with a nice glass of wine to watch a bit of television, the phone rang. It was Lester.

"What?" I blurted.

"It's Brody," he said. "He's gone AWOL."

"Damn it."

"He drove home and checked in with Andrew. Then said he wanted to be alone for a bit and took Andrew to have supper at Debbie's. He told her to drive the kid to the point when he was ready to come back. When Debbie and Andrew got there, Brody and his car were gone and the cottage was locked up tight. Debbie called 911."

"Oh, no. He's going to try to get to Belleville to talk to Carl."

"That won't work. Carl is still out cold and the police down there are aware that Brody may be on his way. They doubled the guard on Carl's room at the hospital and have police all over the place watching for him."

"I feel so bad," I said. "I thought he was okay when he left for home. I thought I'd convinced him to be patient and wait."

"Don't beat yourself up, Hilly. We'll find him. Thought you should know in case he tries to contact you."

"Thanks," I said. "If he calls, but I doubt he will, I'll let you know."

"Use my private cell number if you have to," he said. "And Hilly, make sure all your windows and doors are locked, since we don't know where this Ralph fellow is right now," Lester said. "Have a good night."

"Gee, thanks for reminding me I might have another nocturnal visitor, Lester."

"We all need to be on our toes. Gotta go."

I put the phone down and looked at HD, er, Heidi, who was lying beside me on the sofa. She cocked her head. I patted her. Time for lock patrol I told her. The two of us did a tour of the house checking that all the doors and windows, even the root cellar door, were properly secured. By that time, I had lost interest in television. I finished my wine and my dessert, then went to bed with a book.

I was reading a mystery novel – I enjoy those and normally would have read for quite a while. But I just couldn't concentrate.

I remembered Brody flipping out and trying to get to Belleville. What would he do when he got there? The police wouldn't let him within a mile of Carl. They would probably arrest him. I didn't like to think of my friend spending the night in a cell, not in his frame of mind. It might calm him down, however. Lester could get him out in the morning. I doubted that any charges would be laid, but it was all such a hassle.

Why hadn't Brody listened and just gone home, gotten some sleep?

I knew why. Because I felt much like he probably did: angry and frustrated. His daughter had been put in danger and, right now, he was likely to strike out at anyone who had been involved in the murder and kidnapping.

I thought about what Lester had said in the squad car on the way to the station. We care too much and that makes us dangerous. I was glad my gun was locked up in my office safe. As far as I knew, Brody did not have one. I hoped that was still true.

I dumped the book on the floor and put out the light. I needed my sleep too and besides Lester would let me know if there was any news.

I tossed and turned, eliciting a few grunts from HD, er, Heidi, who now considered half of my bed hers. I would miss her when Zach reclaimed her.

Chapter 17

In my dream, HD was barking up a storm and church bells were ringing. My eyes flew open.

The radio alarm clock said it was 2 a.m.

The barking and ringing were still going on, so I wasn't dreaming.

<u>Barking, HD, oh no not another intruder. They got the file on their second try. Why come back?</u> Or perhaps it was Ralph. I couldn't think straight. I wished the bells would stop ringing. I knew I had to call for help.

Befuddled, I got out of bed and promptly knocked my cell off the nightstand. I blindly groped around for it in the darkened room and luckily found it right away. I was about to dial 911, when my brain said, "hold on that's your doorbell not alarm bells."

Who would be ringing my doorbell at this hour? Lester would have called.

Cautiously I inched over to the bedroom window and looked out. Down below, illuminated by my porch light, was a pickup truck I recognized as Brady's"

I ran downstairs, got HD under control and yanked the door open.

"Hilly, thank god," Brody said. "I need coffee. I have to clear my head."

I stared at him. His face was all agitated, his hair all over the place and he looked like he had dressed in a windstorm. His pants' leg was torn.

"Brody, where on earth have you been? You do realize there's an APB out on you?"

"I figured there might be." He strode into my hallway and I shut the door.

HD had recognized him by now and was licking his hand.

"Good alarm system you got there," Brody said.

"Yeah, I'm thinking of patenting it" I quipped. Then my anger took over. "Brody, what the hell did you think you were doing? Dumping Andrew at his mother's and then taking off like that. The police are on the alert for you all the way down to Bellville. You could have gotten pulled over anywhere, be in jail right now, your truck impounded."

Brody held up a hand. "Enough Hilly I am guilty on all counts. I wasn't thinking clearly."

"And where have you been?" I added. You look like you were rolled in a ditch or something."

"Coffee, Hilly, please. I'll tell all."

"Yes you will," I said, "but first I'm letting Lester know you are here safe and sound.

"Do you have to? I feel kind of foolish about what I did."

"What did you do?" I glared at him. Almost afraid to hear what he had to say.

"As you said, dump off Andrew, lie to my sister and friends and take off in the truck."

"That's it, I swear. I never went anywhere near Belleville."
"That's it?"

I was dialing Lester's private number. "I promised, Lester I'd call if you turned up," I said. "He'll need to call off the alert."

"Okay, okay," Brody said, parking himself at my kitchen table.

A groggy Lester answered the phone. "Hilly, are you okay?"
"I'm fine, Lester, but he's here."

"Who? Ralph?" Lester's voice was suddenly crystal clear and alert.

"No, not Ralph, Brody."

"Brody?"

"He pulled up a few minutes ago and woke me up ringing the doorbell. We're making coffee."

"On my way, hold on a sec. It's okay, Maureen it's okay, go back to sleep – Hilly make enough for three. I'll be there just as soon as I find my damn pants." The line went dead.

"He sound mad?" Brody asked.

"Mad doesn't even come to close to how he feels. Be prepared for a tongue-lashing. And Lester is good at them."

"I know, I know. What I did was kind of stupid."

"Kind of?" I said, measuring coffee grinds into the percolator. Brody looked up and smiled at me weakly. He looked for a moment so much like he did as a young boy when he and Gina and I used to hang out together. Then the care lines and the sadness reappeared.

"Hungry?"

"Maybe."

"Chocolate chip cookies," I offered. Oh boy, if I took that package out of the fridge I'd be in trouble, but hey, anything for my friend.

"I love those. Thanks, Hilly."

I took the cookies out of their hiding place in the back of the fridge. The coffee smell was getting to me now. I brought the bag to the table along with a jug of milk and the sugar bowl. Brody grabbed the bag.

"I don't know why I should be this hungry at what, 2 am?"

"Adrenaline," I said. "It surges through you when you get involved in something and when it's over, you crave food and you need coffee or you'll feel sleepy. You are so lucky you didn't feel asleep at the wheel. Driving around all night like that, so dumb."

"I wasn't driving all the time," Brody said. "Hilly, why are these cookies cold? Do you keep them in the fridge or something?"

"Yeah or I'd be tempted to eat them all in one go," I said.

"What do you mean you weren't driving around all night?"

"Well, I . . . ."

"Hold that thought," I said as the coffemaker started beeping to let me know the coffee was ready. I put it out of its misery and had begun filling two mugs, when Heidi swung into a full barking mode and the bells began ringing in my head again.

Whatever happened to my quiet life in a small seaside town where I could sleep through the night? I might as well be back in the apartment in Roxton with police cars, ambulances, fire engines, heavy trucks and trains filling the night with their cacophony. They used to wake me up all the time. Since I'd moved back to Lamb's Bay, I had been sleeping so well and now this, I thought as I went to answer the door and stop the bell ringing.

Lester bustled in. He greeted the dog who had stopped barking to welcome him. He went straight down the hall to my kitchen. "Where the hell is he?" he roared.

"Right here," Brody said rising from his chair. "Lester, I'm sorry. I wasn't thinking straight."

Lester stared at him. "I figured that part out – the rest? Where the hell did you go to and what did you do?"

"He was just about to tell me so he might as well tell both of us at the same time. Here Lester," I said, handing him a mug of coffee. "Sit down. We're all stressed and tired out."

"I just needed to think," Brody said weakly.

"Think?" Lester grunted. "You couldn't do that back in your own home in your cosy bed? So we all knew where you were? Do you realize . . ." Lester was in full tongue-lashing mode now.

"Do you realize there are police up and down the coastal highway looking for you, not to mention our people and the Bellville force which put extra guards on Carl? You've put a lot of people out tonight with your 'mobile thinking.' Maureen says this keeps up and she's going to her sister's in Fair Haven until this case is closed."

"I'm sorry, Lester, Hilly. I'm sorry." Brody pushed bag of cookies over to me and I tried to ignore it.

"Lester, Brody says he wasn't driving all night like we thought." I eyed the cookies again.

"Then where the hell were you? And you look like a drunk that's been rolled in a ditch."

"That's because I fell down," Brody said.

"Fell? Where?"

Brody took a swig of his coffee. "I know dumping Andrew off and letting Debbie believe I was going straight home for some quiet time was wrong, but I had this need to get away from everyone, especially those trying to help me. I knew they were dealing with the situation in an active way, investigating, etc. But I think I've been in some sort of fugue state since Gina died. Suddenly all the rage about her murder and my fears for Ruby's safety surged through me. I had to get away from everyone and deal with it my own way, so that I could be in a better frame of mind to handle the situation if, and when, Ruby returns."

"And are you?" Lester asked. "In a better frame of mind?"

"I can't really tell, but I feel more clear-headed." He sipped more coffee and pulled the cookie bag back to his side of the table. He pulled one out and then pushed them towards Lester. "Do you know she keeps her cookies in the fridge to stop her from binging on them?"

"Of course," Lester said. "I know these things about people. But what I don't know and what I want to know is an account of your movements this evening."

Brody let out a sigh. "I was angry, confused. I want to let off a string of cuss words, break things. I didn't want Andrew around when I did any of that. So I took him to his mother's for dinner and said they could bring him back later, that I just needed some alone time."

"We know that part," Lester said, scribbling in his ubiquitous notebook. "Go on."

"I really did intend to go back home, but somehow I found my elf and my truck out on the highway. I realized I was headed in the direction of Belleville and I knew I couldn't go there. It wouldn't do any good since this Carl was out cold and the police had him under guard. I didn't have a gun, so I couldn't shoot him and that wouldn't help the case. Dead men take no tales as they say."

Lester glared at Brody over the rim of his cup.

"So," Brody said, "I took the turnoff for Angus Cove."
Angus Cove was a secluded beach surrounded by high cliffs.
The path down to its pristine sandy beach was precarious and
not for those who had trouble with heights. When we were
younger, we often went out there for picnics and bonfires.
During the day, the beach was mostly frequented by
sunbathers and families looking for a quieter place than the
more popular beaches up and down the coast.

"You were at Angus Cove? All this time? Anyone see you
there?"

"There was no one there. I walked on the beach; I railed at the
moon. I threw pebbles into the water and swore. When I ran
out of steam, I sat down on the beach and well," Brody looked
embarrassed. "I cried. I haven't done much of that since Gina
died. I guess it was time it all came out."

I got up and put my arms round Brody's shoulders and gave
him a hug. "Do you really feel better?"

"Like I dumped a sack of stones that were hanging off my
body and weighing me down," he said. "There is still a
heaviness my chest. I don't suppose there's been any news
about Ruby while I was gone?"

"No," Lester said. "But why do you look like that? You
weren't in a scuffle with anyone were you?"

"No," Brody said. "When I finished, you know, ranting, I felt
worn out. I went and sat in my car trying to get myself up to
driving home, but all I wanted to do was sleep, so I let myself
doze off. I woke up needing to pee and, when I got out of the
car to find a convenient bush, the clouds had gone over the
moon and I couldn't see well. Of course, I didn't have a
flashlight. So I kind of stumbled about, still half asleep,
tripped at the top of the path leading to the beach, and fell. I
rolled a ways before I managed to grab a root sticking out of
the ground. Damn near peed myself. I struggled back up the
path, did what I had to do and got back in the car. But I didn't
want to go home to an empty house. So I came here. Plus I
think I need a little first aid."

Brody pointed to his torn pants which I now noticed had a blood stain on them. "Seem to have grazed my kneecap on a rock or something."

"Brody," Lester said. "I think you should stay here for the rest of the night. Can I trust you to do that or I do I have to offer you the hospitality of the local jail so that I can keep tabs on you? I need to go home and sleep – we all need to sleep. Can I trust you to stay put?"

"I'm okay now, Lester," he replied. "Hilly can lend me a first aid kit. Then I can drive home. Hey I got here from Angus Cove didn't I? I promise to stay put there. I sleep better in my own bed."

"We all do," Lester said. But it's better that you stay here. You don't want to go home right now."

"Why?"

"Your sister Debbie and Andrew are camped out there. When she finds out about this night's jaunt, she's going to tear a strip off you. I think you have had enough for now. Get some sleep. I'll be back in the morning. Promise me you'll stay put or I can call the jail." He picked up his cell.

"I'll be good, I promise. I'll sleep here. And Lester, thanks for the warning about Debbie."

"I'll call her in the morning and let her know she can pick you up here. No use waking up all of Lamb's Bay at the same time. Get your knee cleaned up and go to bed."

As I escorted Lester back to the front door, he leaned down and whispered, "Keep him here. I don't need Debbie and her concern over his welfare muddling the situation. He's exhausted anyhow."

"No problem," I said. "The spare room is always made up. But you need to let them know he's all right. And he'll need some clothes."

"I'll let them know and we can address all that in the morning. Meanwhile, I want Sid to go out to Angus Cove first thing and confirm Brody's story."

"You don't believe him"

"I do but it's better if it is documented. Who knows what could happen and I don't want Brody a suspect for something he didn't do."

"What do you mean?"

"Don't tell Brody," Lester told me as we stood on the porch, "but someone tried to get to Carl's room in the hospital in Belleville shortly after his surgery, Dressed as a hospital employee. The man got away. Had to be Ralph. If he had succeeded and the killer got away, given Brody's outburst yesterday, it would have made him a suspect."

"Yikes," I said. "Good job you thought of checking out his story, Lester."

"That's part of the job," he said. "Thinking."

"On that topic," I said, "do you think Ralph and Ruby will stay in the Belleville area because he still wants to kill Carl? Is there any chance he will head up this way?"

"I didn't like to say this in front of Brody, but since they didn't find the gold, and he failed to kill Carl, Ralph's only ace card is Ruby. He may still try a ransom demand. He probably needs cash to finance a getaway. Police are on the lookout for him and not just in this area. His best bet would be to get away by boat, but that takes money. Gas isn't cheap there days. Gotta go. Take care Hilly."

Lester climbed into his car and drove off.

HD had followed me out and was watering my lawn for me. I chided myself for continuing to think of her as HD, reminding myself of the resolve to rename her Heidi. I called her Heidi making it sound like a garbled HD and she actually came back to my side her tail wagging. Hey this could work. We went inside to check on Brody.

He sat at the kitchen table staring into his cup.

"Brody," I said. "You know where the guest room is. There's a spare bathrobe and some towels in the closet. Go and take a shower. The first aid kit is in the bathroom vanity, at the bottom on the right. Do you need me to help with cleaning up your knee?"

"Thanks, Hilly. Lester is right. I am bushed. But I can handle the first aid. You've done enough. Go to bed."

He got up and limped down the hall to the stairs. "You sure me staying over is no problem?"

"If I didn't want guests, I wouldn't have a guest room," I said. "Get."

I tried to settle down in bed with HD, er, Heidi beside me but it was a no go. I heard the shower run for a few minutes and then, after a while, I heard footsteps recede down the hall and the door to the spare room shut. I hoped Brody would have a good long sleep.

Frustrated at not being able to relax enough to doze, I finally got up and decided to take a shower myself. The bathroom was pretty clean given that a man had just used it. Zach had been a messy person in the bathroom, stuff all over the place wet towels on the floor, the toilet seat up. I silently thanked my good friend Gina for having trained Brody properly.

After I got dressed, I went to my office and started doing some work, anything to keep my mind off speculating about Ruby's fate. I got so busy that a couple of hours flew by. Next time I looked up from my screen, it was full daylight and my cell was vibrating.

Chapter 18

"Hi, Hilly," Tracy said. She didn't sound her usual perky self
"What's wrong?" I asked.

"Oh, just woke up. I'm fine, but last night Zach and I had our first big fight in years. He got so upset, the nurse asked me to leave. Claimed I was putting his blood pressure up. I'm probably banned from his hospital room now. No big loss as far as I'm concerned."

"Listen, Tracy, I'm sorry – I guess the fight was about me."

"Oh, that was just the kickoff," Tracy said. "I told him we were on to him and he tried to deny it all. Then he tried the sob story tactic, telling me how much he still loved you, yadda, yadda. I said neither of us was buying that. And that's when he raised his voice. He used that tone, you know, the one he uses when he is putting you down, making you out to be a moron."

"He used to do that to me," I said. "It took me years to understand what he was doing. I was too much in love. But Tracy?"

"Oh, don't worry; I didn't let him get away with it. In fact, I raised my voice and suddenly all the old resentments just came boiling up from the depths. I told him things I've wanted to say for years, since I was a little kid. He thought he was the perfect brother but he wasn't."

"Ouch, Tracy."

"Yeah, well, he didn't like hearing all that, especially when I told him I knew why he'd tried to scam you."

"Why? I have to admit I wondered about that after all this time."

"He's turning 40 in a couple of weeks. He lives alone. He works crazy hours and travels. He probably decided it was time he had a woman around all the time to take care of him and the apartment and the dog. So he thought he could just step back into your life. When I told him that, he threw his water jug at me and rang for the nurse."

"Oh my god, did he hit you?"

Tracy laughed. "He could never hit the side of a barn. That's why I played baseball and he didn't. Hilly, don't feel bad. It really had nothing to do with you. I think I've just been waiting for an excuse to start the conversation with him, to tell him about everything that's bothered me for years. And you know, I feel wonderful today."

"Wonderful, Tracy, but you sound exhausted."

"Nope, I slept like a lamb. Hung over might be more like it."

You, Tracy? Hung over? I've never seen you drink enough to get hung over."

"I certainly did last night. Norm is out of town camping with the boys so I went home, ordered a pizza, opened a nice bottle of red and had my way with it."

"Wow," I said.

"Definitely wow. Zach called a couple of times, but I didn't pick up. I've decided he's too toxic for me. You had the right idea, Hilly, to get out of town and leave him. I told Norm all about it when he called this morning."

"What was his response?"

"He said it was about time. Way to go, Tracy." She laughed. "Norm is a great guy and Zach never liked him. I think it was because he could see through Zach's bullshit. They were polite to each other, but give Norm a choice between spending time with Zach or a grizzly bear, I think Norm would prefer the bear."

I laughed. "Tracy, I'm glad you got it out of your system. Heck, if I knew years back that you needed to do that, I'd have unloaded on you back then."

"I probably couldn't have handled it back then," she said. "But now – I am Tracy, hear me roar."

We both dissolved into giggles.

"So, on a more sober note, how are things up there?" she asked.

Back to reality. I gave her the shorthand version of what had happened since we last spoke.

"So Brody spent the night at your place," she asked.

"That's what you got out of all that" I asked. "Murder, kidnapping, police raids, a shooting and all you focused on was the fact that I had an overnight guest?"

"Yeah, yeah I got the bit about what happened." Her voice got huskier. "But Hilly, having a man in the house? He's an old friend right? Do you like him? Does he fancy you?"

"Tracy, get out of romance novel mode. Brody's wife was murdered a few days ago; his daughter is missing. Yes we are old friends, but there's no romance here."

"Duh," she said. "We'll see. There's always the old 'comforting the widower plot.' Well, gotta go. Hang in there, Hilly."

Honestly, that girl was always trying to read romance into situations where it did not belong. I guess that's what made her successful at writing her books. But she had to realize that Brody and I were just friends.

HD, who appeared to be getting used to her new name, Heidi, got up and padded towards the doorway, her tail wagging. I looked over and saw Brody wearing a bathrobe and standing there looking kind of lost.

"Morning, Hilly. Um, can I borrow a pair of sweatpants? My pants kind of smell bad."

"And look worse," I said. "I'll go root out a pair. Put on some coffee will you? There's muffins in the fridge."

He shuffled off down the hallway and I ran upstairs to find my largest sweat pants, the ones I liked to lounge around in when I was in a super lazy mood. The thought of Brody wearing them kind of made me blush a little. <u>Hilly, he's just a good friend. He's mourning. Stop it. Tracy is bad enough, but you too?</u>

About an hour later, the doorbell rang. Heidi was out in the garden but I could hear her barking. It was Debbie and, if anyone was loaded for bear, she was.

She stalked into the house, barely greeting me. "Brody," she called, her voice starting to rise.

Brody stuck his head out of the kitchen door and ducked back in. He knew she was upset.

I accompanied her into the kitchen. "Why don't you two talk in the garden," I suggested. "Brody, get Debbie some coffee."

"I don't want any coffee," she growled. "Now about last night."

Brody walked out the back door followed by Debbie. The barking stopped, thank goodness. I went back to my office and closed the window. I didn't want to hear the conversation, if it could be called that, between Debbie and Brody. She had a sharp tongue when she was angry and, even if Lester had managed to diffuse the situation, Brody was still in hot water with his big sister.

Sitting at my desk, I put some music on and donned my headphones. I tried hard to concentrate on my work, but the image of Tracy giving Zach heck after all these years hovered in front of my eyes. Good for her. I'd done the same thing before I left him. People like Zach were toxic like she'd said and they were better out of our lives.

I sighed and went back to working on a client's file. After all, I had lost enough time working on this case with Lester and, since my consultant job paid in coffee and doughnuts, I had to get some "real" work done to pay my bills.

Between the music and work, I got so involved that I didn't hear Brody trying to talk to me until he lifted one of the earphones off and said "Helloo?" Loudly.

"Brody," I said. "You scared me."

"Just wanted to let you know we are leaving." He was wearing a pair of his own pants and a polo shirt with the windbreaker he had been wearing when he arrived.

"You need to wash that jacket," I said.

"Debbie has already pointed that out. Thank you for letting me stay and get some sleep, Hilly, and for everything you've done. I'm really worry I got you mixed up in all this."

"Gina was my friend," I said. "I would have gotten mixed up in it anyway."

"True," Brody said.

"Where's Debbie?"

"In the bathroom."

"You two work things out?"

"I talked, she yelled, she got it out of her system. We're okay now."

Debbie and Brody, such a different brother-sister dynamic from Zach-Tracy.

"She'll drive me home. Andrew is holding the fort right now. Don't want to leave him on his own too long."

"He seems pretty reliable," I said.

Brody nodded. "I guess he is. I just remember what I was like at that age."

"Pretty crazy," I said.

Brody smiled sadly. "Gina always said she fell in love with me back then. I wish now she hadn't waited until we were in our twenties to tell me."

"She always thought she wasn't good enough for you," I said. "That some beauty queen would come along and claim you."

Brody shook his head. "I always went for the smart ones, not the empty-headed Barbie dolls. Gina was a smart woman and beautiful, too. Hilly, I can't talk about her any more. It hurts too much."

"Brody?" Debbie voice cut into our conversation. "Oh hi, Hilly."

"Hi, Debbie. Thanks for picking him up," I said. "Saved me a drive."

Debbie smiled. "Thanks for the private time to off steam in the garden. I love your dog by the way. She's so affectionate once she stops treating you like a burglar. When does she get her stitches out?"

"In a couple more days."

"Come on, Brody," Debbie said. "Let the woman work."

I walked them to the front door and waved goodbye as they drove off. Then I locked it securely and went to rescue Heidi from the back yard. Looking at the clock, I realized it was lunchtime for both of us.

It was late afternoon when the cellphone vibrated again. I was busy and didn't really feel like being disturbed so I checked the screen before answering. It was Lester.

"What's up?" I said.

"Brody still there?"

"No," I said. "He left at lunch time. Debbie brought him some clothes and then drove him home."

"She give him hell about last night?"

"And then some. I was diplomatic I did not listen. I sent them out into the garden, then went into my office and listed to music through my headphones. I didn't need to be privy to that conversation."

Lester chuckled. "When I spoke to her this morning, Debbie was half glad he was okay and half raging mad he was such an idiot."

"Big sisters," I said. "Any other news?"

Lester told me that one of his officers had been out to Angus Point and confirmed there were signs a car was parked out there recently. "The tire treads look like they belong to Brody's truck. I'm having that checked."

"I'm still surprised you wanted to check out Brody's story, Lester."

"Hilly, there's been enough weirdness in this case so I'm checking everything. There were also footprints on the beach and places where it looked like someone had kicked rocks around. And urine on one of the bushes near where the truck was parked. So for now I'm presuming Brody told the truth." I asked if there was any news from Belleville.

"Apparently Carl has asked for a lawyer and wants a deal. The police told him Ralph tried to get to him last night and he's scared for his life. Says he didn't sign on for all this. He'll talk and tell all, but he doesn't want to be charged in Gina and Janet's murders. He'll talk in return for lesser charges."

"Is that going to work?" I asked

"Lawyers are working on it," Lester replied. "If it was up to me, well . . ."

"He just got shot in the leg, Lester. It would be cruel to throw him up against a wall. This isn't the wild west."

"Wow, you think I'd do that, Hilly?" he asked.

"Heck, if it would solve the case, I would but we both know we can't operate like that."

"For sure," he said. "I'll let you know if there's more news." I caught up on a lot of work and then decided to take Heidi for a walk. I wanted to get away from everything for a while. The day had turned out fair, but there was a cool wind blowing in off the sea. Heidi and I drove out to the beach and we rambled for about an hour. I like wind. I blows the cobwebs out of your mind, clears out your lungs. You feel invigorated after a brisk walk along the seashore. And that's how I was feeling when Heidi and I arrived back at the house. As I boiled water for a cup of tea, I reflected on how fairly normal today had been compared to the previous days this week.

Tracy had finally cut her ties with Zach. Brody and Debbie had cleared the air about him taking off last night. I'd gotten a head start on some of my client work. No one had tried to break into my house or shoot anyone.

I just wished I knew what was going on down in Belleville with Carl. I knew how Lester felt about the lawyer business. He always said, "Involve the lawyers and you'll never get anything done." Well I guess in this situation, we'd have to wait until Carl got his deal worked out. But I hoped Ralph wouldn't try anything dangerous in the coming hours.

If Carl could tell us what he planned, Lester and his men might be able to track him down and capture him. Of course, there was Ruby to consider. The poor girl was probably frightened out of her wits and confused to boot. She had looked odd in the blurry photo Janet had left in my mailbox. I still thought her kidnappers were giving her some kind of drug to keep her quiet. She couldn't help them find the missing gold but they wanted to use her as a bargaining chip. If so, when we finally got her home, and I prayed that she came home safely, she would not remember much of her ordeal. That would be a good thing for Ruby. However, there still remained the fact that she probably witnessed her mother's murder.

I knew Ruby would need professional help and wondered if perhaps Brody might benefit from some too. He'd had his night on the beach working out his emotions, but was that enough to allow him to get back to some semblance of a normal life? Though after what happened to Gina and Ruby, I doubted if life would ever be normal again for him and his daughter.

The kettle boiled and I pulled out the plug. I poured the water into a big mug that contained a bag of my favorite herbal tea. I had just settled down on the back porch with Heidi at my side when the cellphone started to vibrate again.

What now I thought. Uh oh, it was Lester, again.

"Hilly, we may have a problem. You said Brody went home right? Do you know if Andrew is with him?"

"He said Andrew was going to continue staying with him – anything to keep Debbie off his back."

"He's not answering his phone. And Carl's been talking. The Belleville police told me he said Ralph was planning to head up here and to use Ruby as leverage to get Brody to tell him where the gold is. He's convinced both Gina and Brody knew more about it. "

"Oh my god" I said. "What do you need me to do?"

"I think you might be in danger too," Lester said. "So I'd prefer it if you came in and stayed at the station for now. I'll send a squad car to – wait a minute." He put me on hold.

I sat there with my motor in high gear. I needed to be doing something to help out, not sitting here on hold.

Lester came back on the phone. "Hilly?"

"Yes?"

"Bad news. Andrew just called from the rental cottage office. He says a man with a gun showed up with Ruby. Andrew was just coming up from the jetty on the cliff path when he saw the man forcing Brody into the house and dragging Ruby with him. Andrew didn't have his phone with him, so he hightailed it down to the boat and rowed over to the rental office to use that phone to call us."

"Damn it," I said. "Did you tell Andrew to stay put? To keep the rowboat there?"

"Of course, why?"

"If we drive onto the point, Ralph will see the police car right away. But if you and your men row a boat over to the jetty on the point – there's two more moored at the rental office — you can get up to the house via the cliff path. Ralph can't see that path from the house."

"Good idea, Hilly, Lester said. "I want you to stay put."

"Fat chance, Lester," I said. "I'm closer than you are – I'll meet you there."

I hung up over Lester's protests. I ran to my office and retrieved my gun from my safe. Then I sprinted out the front door, leaving Heidi in command of the house, and drove like a bat out of hell all the way to the rental office.

Chapter 19

I pulled into a parking space in front of the rental office.
Andrew was waiting for me.

"Are the cops coming, Hilly" he asked.

"They are on their way. Andrew, did you call your mother?"

"Are you kidding?" Andrew asked "If I told her what was
going on, she'd make me come home. I'm staying put."
Andrew's face was lit up by a mixture of excitement and
anxiety. He could barely stand still. He was pacing like his
Uncle Brody. "We have to do something, Hilly."

I grabbed him by the shoulders and turned him to face me.
"Going home until this is all over might be a better idea," I
said.

Andrew shook his head. "Not until they are safe," he said.

I knew a bit about how long hostage situations could take to
resolve. I also knew how fast they could fall apart and end
tragically. "This could take a while, Andrew. You should go
home."

He pulled away from me. "I'm not a baby, Hilly. That's my
uncle and my cousin over there with the crazy guy. I'm
staying put and I want to help in any way I can."

Great, just what Lester and his men needed. A gung-ho
teenager who wanted to be a hero. I dropped my hands and
turned as I heard a car pulling in. Lester, Harry and Sid had
arrived.

Lester walked right over to Andrew. I stepped back to give
him space. "That was quick thinking to come over here and
call us," Lester said. But I want you to go home and take Hilly
with you. Both of you need to stay out of the way, you hear?"

"Sure," Andrew said, "unless you need my help that is. I do
know the point like the back of my hand." He gave Lester a
smile full of eagerness to get involved.

Lester turned to me. "Hilly?"

"Of course, we'll stay out of the way," I said.

"Somehow, I don't believe you or him," Lester said, pointing at Andrew. "I have no desire for Debbie to rip out my heart if anything happens to either of you. Stay put."

The three cops piled into one of the rowboats and set off across the cove to the jetty on the side of the point. It was a short trip and within a few minutes, we saw them moor the boat and start climbing the rocky path. I just prayed that Ralph was still inside the cottage so he could not see them either.

Andrew was pacing again. "Hilly, we have to do something. The way that man was waving his gun around, he was really angry. I heard him shout at Uncle Brody that if someone didn't tell him where the gold was, people would start dying."

I wasn't happy to hear that. An armed man is one thing. An armed man who is losing it is even worse. And it sounded as if Ralph was definitely losing it. He must have been crazy to come back here, knowing that all the cops in this area were looking for him. Of course, if he hadn't come back, he wouldn't have had a use for Ruby and she would probably be dead by now. Catch 22.

"We have a chance to save them," I said. "It will be all right, Andrew. Stop that pacing and come and sit down. Lester is a good cop and knows what he is doing. He and Harry and Sid will save them, I'm sure."

"I'm not," Andrew said. "I can't sit still and do nothing. I'm going over there. Perhaps I can help out by making a distraction or, or something."

"You've been watching too many action shows and movies," I told him. "People who try to distract armed gunmen often end up dead or wounded. The gunmen don't want to deal with a distraction. So they shoot the person. From what I know, and from what you told me Ralph said, he is near the breaking point. Instead of being distracted by you, he is more likely to shoot you and Ruby as well. Even your Uncle Brody."

"Then what can we do?" Andrew asked.

"We stay put and . . ."

"No way," Andrew said. "If you won't come with me, I'm going alone. I want to help." He started down towards the other row boat.

"Andrew," I called running after him. "Wait." I knew I couldn't let him go alone. Debbie would have my head if one hair on Andrew's body was missing when he returned home. I climbed into the boat with him and, as he rowed us over to the point, I held forth on what the rules would be. "No getting in the way of the cops. No trying to provide a distraction. No making any kind of noise that could attract attention to the police. Staying well back from the action and, particularly, making sure that Ralph did not know we were there."

"Yeah, yeah," he whispered as he tied up the boat. "Keep your voice down Hilly, Noise carries around here." He jumped out onto the jetty and I followed a little bit slower. He was about to begin climbing the path when I caught up with him.

"One more rule," I said. "I go first."

"Why?" he protested.

"Because I'm the grownup, I know what I am doing and, besides, I say so," I hissed.

Andrew made a sound halfway between a growl and a laugh. "Sure thing, Hilly."

I didn't rise to the bait. I made a mental note to discuss that comment with him later and started up the path, wishing that those around me would take me seriously. I did know what I was doing. At least I thought I knew.

We met Lester and his men two-thirds of the way up the path. They were trying to figure out the best approach to the situation.

"What the hell, Hilly?" Lester whispered. "I gave you strict instructions not to come over here."

"It's my fault," Andrew said. "I started to row over and she jumped into the boat to stop me and well, er, . . ."

"You overpowered her?"

"Yes," Andrew said, giving me a look that said "play along please."

I was stunned. What would Andrew come out with next? He repeated, "I overpowered her and made her come with me."

Lester glared at both of us. "Debbie is going to ground you, Andrew, when this is over and I'm going to ground Hilly. Got that?" he hissed.

We both nodded.

"So what's the plan," I asked.

"I called Roxton from the car to get the SWAT team over here," Lester said, "but it will take them up to 20 minutes, half an hour to get here. They have to land their helicopter on the mainland or Ralph will see it and know they are coming. Meanwhile, I'll try talking to him, bargain with him. See if we can buy time." His whispery voice trailed off into silence.

"The meanwhile is what has me worried," I said. "What's the situation right now?"

"Harry managed to slip up to the cottage wall and peer in the living room window without being seen. Ralph had his back to the window luckily. Brody is tied to a chair Ruby is just sitting quietly on the sofa rocking. Ralph was screaming that they had to tell him where the gold was or he'd start shooting body parts."

I shuddered. "Poor kid, poor Brody. Andrew is right; we do have to do something. Lester, do you really think talking to him will help at all? We can't just wait for a SWAT team to get here."

"We also don't have the manpower right now to storm the place and you and I both know what the risks are in that kind of operation. If we could separate Ralph from Brody and Ruby, they might stand a better chance. Anyone got any suggestions?"

The three policemen were whispering away, going over possible scenarios when I butted in. "I have an idea," I said. Three heads swiveled my way.

"Ralph doesn't know we are all here yet, right?"

They all nodded

So why don't I just go knock on the door, pretend like I just arrived by rowboat to visit."

Lester shook his head. "Then he'll take you hostage, too. No way."

"He knows who I am and that I had copies of all Gina's file. I'll tell him I figured out where the gold is and I'll show him if he'll let them go."

"He's not stupid, Hilly," Lester said. "He won't let them go. He would just plan on killing three people instead of two."

"But, wait," I said. "You stay hidden. I'll suggest he locks Ruby and her father in the cottage while I show him where the gold is. Then you can rescue them while I lure him away."

"But you don't know where the gold is."

"No one does," I said. "But Ralph doesn't know that."

"I don't see a positive outcome," Lester said. "When he realizes you are taking him on a wild goose chase, he'll shoot you and then go back and kill the others."

I shook my head. "No he won't because by then, you will have rescued Brody and Ruby. Meanwhile, Harry and Sid can come after us and find a way to overpower Ralph and save me."

"What do you guys think," Lester asked his men.

"Works for me," Harry said. Sid nodded

"Lester, I'll take him down the path below the lighthouse that leads to the beach. There's lots of tricky footing there so it will take us some time to get down to that narrow strip of beach. There's a couple of caves down there and I can let him think one of them hides the gold. He'll be so intent on getting there, they'll have a chance to jump him from behind."

Lester sighed. "I hope for your sake Hilly that this all works. You know he might not go for any of it. Might just shoot you and get it over with."

"No, he has gold fever. He needs to find that treasure and he'll grab at anything that will help him to get it. Brody doesn't know anything; Ruby is no help so I'll be it."

Lester looked long and hard at me, then said. "We'll take a chance, good luck, Hilly."

A few minutes later, I finished climbing the path to the cottage. My heart was hammering in my chest, my palms were sweaty and I was wondering if I really had lost all sense of reality. After all, in the heat of the moment, I had volunteered to talk an armed gunman out of two hostages in exchange for me showing him where the gold was. I must be nuts. I stood looking around as if I was admiring the view instead of trying to get control of my feelings.

Calm, Hilly. This is for Brody and Ruby. This is for Gina.

I took a deep breath and walked over to the cottage's front door. I knocked. "Brody, you home?" I reached for the doorknob, turned it and pushed the door open. I mentally crossed my fingers that this would work.

A man with a gun pointed right at my chest stood in the middle of the room. Brody sat tied to a chair, blood on his face and his eyes closed. Ruby was humming to herself on the sofa.

"Who are you," the man growled. "What do you want?"

"Ralph?" I asked.

His eyes narrowed. "You guessing? You police."

"No," I said. "Not the police. I thought I could perhaps help us both out."

"Help out with what?" He walked closer to me and stared intently. "You're that woman."

"The one you stole Gina's file from," I said.

"Huh," he said. "Nasty dog you got. Did I kill it?"

"No, just nicked her ear. Look, Ralph . . . "

"Get over here," he said, waving his gun towards the sofa. "Sit." I sat

"What do you want? You sure you didn't bring the cops?" He backed over to the window and looked outside. All was apparently clear as far as he was concerned because he turned back to face the three of us.

"Now I will only ask one more time. What are you doing here?"

"Carl said you were on your way here to see Brody. You wanted to find the gold."

Ralph looked surprised. I had his attention now.

"Carl? How do you know Carl? He's dead anyway."

"Unfortunately not," I said. "I heard through my contacts that he made a deal with the cops and he's telling all"

"Son of a bitch," Ralph snarled. "And just where do you fit in all this?"

"I'm a researcher," I said. "Gina hired me to help her track down the gold. But," I shrugged, "she died before I could tell her where it is." I waved a hand at Brody. "You wasted your time with this one. He didn't know a thing. His wife never told him what she was doing. I'm the one who knows."

"And you are going to keep that secret to yourself or perhaps tell me?" He waved his gun in front of me."

"I'll tell you," I said, "if you stop threatening me with that gun. And if you agree to my terms."

"Terms? Listen lady, I'm the one with the gun." He stuck it right in front of my face.

"And I'm the one who knows where the gold is. Sounds like a standoff to me."

Ralph looked me up and down, assessing me. He stared without blinking. I stared back. Inside, I was quaking, but he didn't need to know that.

"So lady," he said, taking a few steps back and pointing the gun away from me. "What are you terms?"

"I have a boat down at the jetty. I can take you to where the gold is stashed, but I need help getting it to the boat. Right now, no one knows you are here. And if we keep those two quiet, we'll have time to get away with at least part of the gold."

Ralph looked at me suspiciously. "Why not all of it?" he asked.

"10 gold bars are heavy, but if you think we can do it, I'm game," I replied.

"So what? You want me to shoot those two so they can't talk?"

I shook my head. "Another two murders would really make the cops hotter than ever on your trail and mine. We'd both have real trouble getting away with this. Better to lock them in here, inside the cottage. The girl doesn't talk or use the phone – you can cut the cord – and he's out cold. Tape his mouth shut so that if he does wake up he can't call out."

"I like your thinking, missy," Ralph said. "Sounds like you've done stuff like this before?"

I shrugged. "My past is my secret. You in or out?"

Ralph studied my face again for a few minutes. The clock on the mantle ticked away. Would he buy it?

"I'm in," he said. "Where is the gold?"

"It's not far from here," I said.

"On the point?"

I nodded. "Of course. In a cave."

"We checked out all those caves, even dove into some that are now under water. Nada. I don't believe you."

I smiled. "Ralph, I grew up playing on the point with him." I jerked my head in Brody's direction. "And Gina, that woman you killed." My throat caught at the mention of her name and I almost lost it, but I steeled myself to stay in character. "We had all sorts of hiding places. Once Gina collected all the clues and information, it wasn't hard for me to figure out which cave and which hiding place to look in. I found it two days ago. Been keeping it quiet. Thought I'd keep it for myself, but I couldn't move it all as I said. So I'm willing to go 60-40."

"60-40 – are you insane? It's 50-50 or no deal."

"Okay, 50-50 – no matter to me. Just one of those bars will set my retirement fund up really well. Five will let me plan some beach time in a warmer climate."

 I looked at my watch. "Better get moving. It is getting late."

Ralph nodded. He pulled a roll of duct tape out of his jacket pocket and deftly stuck it across Brody's mouth. Brody stirred, his eyes fluttered and then closed again. Good, didn't need him to see me standing here bargaining with Ralph.

"What about her," he said. "Should we tie her up, too? She might let her father loose."

"Nah," I said. "Let's put her in the bathroom and jam the door shut. She won't be able to figure out how to get out."

I went over and took Ruby hand. She seemed really out of it and I suspected Ralph had given her something to keep her quiet and easy to handle.

"Come on," I said. "Time to go to the bathroom." Ruby stared at me then got up and followed me over to the bathroom door. Once she was inside, Ralph jammed a chair under the handle locking her in.

"So, let's go," he said. "What are doing now?"

I was rummaging in a cupboard under the stairs. "Just getting this," I said pulling out a knapsack. "We need something to carry the gold in."

Ralph gave me a half smile and nodded. "You are a smart lady."

"And I hope to be a rich one soon," I said.

"Maybe," Ralph said, smiling again. "Maybe."

I knew that his plan was to let me show him where the gold bars were, then kill me and use my boat as part of his getaway. My plan was to lure him down to the beach where Harry and Sid were waiting to capture him. I was betting my plan would work. I didn't like thinking about his.

\

Chapter 20

Ralph cautiously opened the front door. "You sure there are no cops around?"

"Positive," I said. "The chief called me earlier to say he and his men were heading down to Belleville to interview Carl. We're alone on the point."

"Let's go," he said.

I led the way towards the lighthouse. Ralph followed me and I was acutely conscious of the fact he had a gun and could shoot me in the back at any moment. As we neared the lighthouse, I couldn't help thinking about Chrissie's story in her journal. How Dan and Elmont had attacked Myron and tied him up, leaving him in the lighthouse while they went to hide their loot.

We passed the lighthouse station and turned left towards the edge of the cliff. We were near the place where Gina was probably attacked by Ralph and his gang and thrown over the cliffs into the sea. I shuddered and felt cold sweat trickle down my back.

"Why you shaking?" Ralph asked.

"It's a cold wind," I replied. "I should have brought a jacket."

"Too bad," he said. "Don't worry, once we sell the gold you can buy all the jackets you want."

<u>Sure, that's if I survive.</u>

He waved his gun at the path which led down the cliff to the beach.

"We going down there?" he said. "We looked in the caves down there."

"Ah, but not with someone who knows the point. I, er, suggest you put that gun away," I added.

"No way," he said.

"Just a suggestion but you'll find it difficult to hold on to while we descend this path. There's a rope handrail on both sides and, believe me, it is steep enough that you need to hold on with both hands."

He snorted. "Doesn't bother me, lady," he said. "Get going."

"It's best if you go down facing the cliff," I said, "as if you were climbing down a ladder." I turned around, grabbed the ropes and started my descent.

Ralph followed.

The path was precarious and I had to concentrate on not putting a foot wrong or I could find myself tumbling straight down. If I fell into the water, I had a chance of surviving, but not if I fell straight down onto the rocky beach. That's what had happened to Gina. I kept hoping that Harry and Sid had their side of the plan all organized.

We were ten feet from the bottom of the path when I heard Ralph swear and looked up to see him slip sideways. He managed to recover, but he needed both hands for that and, in the struggle to maintain his equilibrium he lost his hold on the gun. It went spiralling over my head down into a pile of rocks on the beach below.

Whew. Great. Now he was unarmed and he didn't know that I was armed and that there were two police officers nearby.

As I reached the beach, I looked around but could see no trace of the two men. I was getting nervous. Had something happened to them? Had they changed the plan? Had the SWAT team turned up early and revised the plan? What next? All I could think was that I couldn't let Ralph get his hands on his gun again. I had to take the upper hand.

Ralph reached the bottom of the path and was wheezing like crazy. "What a climb," he said.

"I heard tell you were a diver, I said, playing for time. "Aren't you guys supposed to be in great shape?"

"I am in great shape," he replied, "but that slip was a bit much. Where the hell did my gun go to anyway? I think it fell over here." He started towards the small cluster of rocks where the gun had fallen. Still no sign of Harry and Sid. I had to act.

"Hold it," I said, pulling my gun out of my purse. "Don't move."

"What the . . .," he roared. He took two steps towards me.

"Don't even try it, mister," I said. "I'll shoot."

Ralph stopped moving and started balefully at me. "I thought we had a deal."

"We do," I said.

"So why the gun and do you even know how to use that thing?" He took a small step towards me.

"Stop," I said. "I know to use this and I think I'm a better shot than you."

He smiled and took another step towards me. "I don't think you'll shoot me," he said. "I'm a nice guy. I offered to help you get the gold away from here."

It was my turn to snort. "I believe it was I who offered you the chance to volunteer your help."

He laughed softly and took another step. I didn't like the way this was turning out. Harry and Sid should have been here by now. Where was my back up? Ralph was calling my bluff. He was slowly edging closer and closer. I'd be forced to shoot him.

"Stop right now," I said.

"Make me." He kept inching forward.

I took the safety off the gun and aimed at the centre of his chest. "I'm warning you, I'll shoot."

"No, you won't," he said.

Suddenly he made a quick move towards me and I squeezed the trigger. The hammer fell on an empty cylinder. "Oh, crap." I had emptied the gun as usual when I stored it in my safe and in my haste to go and meet Andrew, I hadn't stopped to pick up ammunition and load it.

Ralph laughed and made a dive for me. I did the only thing I could. I threw my gun in his face and ran like hell.

I ran as fast as I could which is no mean feat on sand. I heard Ralph pounding along behind me so I pushed myself to keep moving. My lungs were bursting. I felt a giddy but I kept pumping my legs as fast as I could. It was that or get killed. The sound of the waves hitting the rocky outcrop ahead of me filled my ears. But there was another sound all of a sudden – gunshots.

I paused to look back and saw that Harry and Sid had finally turned up. They had Ralph face down on the beach. Thank god. I flopped down on the sand and fought to get my breathing under control. I made a mental note to exercise more.

A few minutes later, Harry came over to check on me. When he'd seen me flop down, he thought I'd been hit by a stray bullet. "We only fired warning shots when we saw he was unarmed," she said apologetically.

"I'm fine," I said, "but what the heck took you guys so long?"

"It's embarrassing," she said.

"What's embarrassing? All you had to do was climb down here and set up an ambush."

"Yeah, well it turns out Sid has a problem with heights."

"With heights?"

"He took one look at that steep path and almost lost his cookies. So we back tracked to the rowboat with Andrew and had him row us over here. That's what held us up. He dropped us off around the headland and we got here as fast as we could. Sorry."

I stared at her. "Sorry? I almost got shot."

"Ah, but you didn't," Harry pointed out. "And we got our man."

"What? Now you're a Mountie?" I asked.

Harry laughed. "We radioed Lester. Brody and Ruby are safe and someone is coming by boat to get us. If you are that knocked out from running, just lie there and take some deep breaths. You'll be fine."

"Oh, gee thanks," I said, still panting.

"Hilly, you might want to take up jogging if you are going to keep on getting involved in police cases," Harry said. "Just a thought."

"Oh yes, thank you, very nice," I said. "Just a thought."

She laughed and started to walk back to where Sid was keeping a close eye on Ralph.

"Wait a minute " I called. "Ralph's gun. I think it fell into that rock pile over there. He dropped it as we were coming down the path. It is probably the one he shot Carl with."

"Thanks, Hilly," Harry said and jogged over to the rock pile.

A few minutes later she waved and shouted, "Got it."

I lay back on the beach assessing my situation to see if there were any other loose ends to worry. The only one I could come up with was the location of the missing gold which was still, er, missing. And probably would be forever. Personally, I was convinced it had never been on Paxton Point. After all, as children we had explored all the caves. Lots of treasure hunters had done the same. The result – no treasure. As Brody said, the only treasures on the point had been his wife and his daughter Ruby

About 15 minutes later, a police launch turned up to take myself, Harry, Sid and an extremely unhappy Ralph back to the rental office beach where a squad car waited.

Andrew was there, jabbering away to members of the SWAT team who had turned up, but now found they weren't really needed. I think he was trying to get information on what studies you had to do get hired for a SWAT team. Debbie would have a fit.

I was tired and still emotional from my ordeal, but my mind immediately turned to the question of how Brody and Ruby were.

"They are being checked out at the hospital," Andrew told me. "Hilly, you were so brave."

"Yes, I was," I said surprising myself at the satisfaction I felt about my role in the rescue of Brody and Ruby, as well as Ralph's arrest.

Andrew went on talking and took me down a peg. "SWAT team thinks you were stupid. Should have waited for them. Think you put yourself in jeopardy unnecessarily."

I waved off his words. "Oh, they're just pissed off because we wrapped it all up without them."

"Yeah, I'd say that about sums it up," Lester said, strolling over. "You okay? Need to go to the hospital, get checked out?"

"No, I'm fine," I said. "I got more exercise this afternoon than I do in a week – though I guess that's not really true since I have to walk Heidi all the time."

"Who's Heidi," Lester asked.

"The dog," I said. "I changed her name. HD was ridiculous."

"Good move," Lester said. "Why use initials for a dog's name anyway?"

"I know why and I'll explain it all, but some other time. I need to go home, take a bath, eat a meal, drink wine and sleep. After I walk the dog."

Lester smiled. "Off you go. I'll get a full statement from you in the morning. Now I got to go and process this guy and it's going to be a lot of paperwork and co-ordination with the other police forces involved. Gonna be a long night. Think when this all calms down, I should take Maureen away for a vacation – either that or she'll divorce me."

I patted Lester on the shoulder and smiled. "She wouldn't divorce you, Lester," I said. "She loves you."

He blushed a bit then smiled back. "She does. And I love her."
He cleared his throat and changed the topic back to my
welfare. "You sure you are okay on your own?"
"Fine," I said, "except for one thing."
"What's that?"
"Get Andrew home will you before he runs away with the
SWAT team."
Lester chuckled. "He's a keener all right. I'll square it all away
with Debbie. See you later."
I drove slowly home via the chicken take-out restaurant and
picked up a dinner. Despite my recent resolve to cook more
for myself, I had neither the inclination nor the energy to
manage kitchen duties that night. This time, however, I would
make sure the dog got nowhere near my food.
It helped that Heidi was anxiously awaiting me. She ran out to
water the lawn and then came right back inside showing a
marked interest in my chicken dinner. But I kept it far away
from her.
"No way," I said. "Eat your kibble."
I poured myself a large glass of wine, then I took her food
bowl, my wine and the chicken dinner, still in its cardboard
box, out onto the back porch. I took pity on Heidi and poured
some of the gravy onto her kibble which she appreciated. We
ate while the sun dipped towards the horizon.
Just another afternoon in Lamb's Bay. Quiet, cosy Lamb's Bay,
where nothing ever happened. Sure thing.
After a warm bubble bath and another glass of my favorite
chardonnay, I was in my PJs and thinking about heading for
an early night when the phone rang.
Now what? I picked up the phone and checked the screen. I
did not recognize the number and debated answering it. If it
was Zach again, I was not interested in hearing from him. I
could tell by the area code it was a Roxton number. It was
about to go to voice mail when I took a deep breath and
answered.
"Hilly."

I recognized the voice immediately, despite its tone of exhaustion. "Brody. Where are you?"

I'm still at the hospital in Roxton, so is Ruby. They transferred us down here. Ruby had some drugs in her system. She's also going to need some psychological help that we don't have up in Lamb's Bay. I, well you know I got roughed up by that cretin, Ralph."

"I know," I said. I closed my eyes and visualized poor Brody tied to that chair, unconscious with blood dripping down his face.

"Hilly, I just spoke with the police. They told me what happened. Hilly, you were so brave and so crazy."

"That's me," I quipped, "brave and crazy."

"Don't joke," Brody said. "You saved our lives by bargaining with that man. How did you do that? Weren't you scared? I really thought he was going to kill both myself and Ruby."

"Honestly, Brody, I don't really remember every detail. One minute I was worried about you two and the next I had volunteered to go in there and bargain for your lives. I can only say I did it for the love I have for both of you. And I'm glad it worked out."

"So am I," Brody said. "That madman was all set to beat me to death, to do all kinds of unmentionable things to Ruby to get me to tell where the gold was hidden and he would not believe that I didn't know."

"I think that's why he accepted my offer so eagerly," I said. "He was highly frustrated by not being able to find it and very angry that even you did not know where it was. When I offered him a solution, he jumped at the chance.

"But it was so dangerous."

If I really had shown him where the gold was, it would have been a lot more dangerous. I knew he would kill me and go back and kill you two. Then take the gold for himself. Luckily our plan to ambush him worked."

Brody sighed. "All that research Gina did which got her killed and no one is any closer to finding out where the gold went to," he said. "It really is a mystery."

"I don't think it was ever on Paxton Point" I said. "The police searched the point back in the thirties. Treasure hunters had a go at finding it over the years and, from what Gina's research shows, so did some Paxton family members. It never showed up. It is either buried somewhere else, known only to Dan, or it was on the point and, when one of the sea caves collapsed due to earth tremors, it got lost. It could be buried either in solid rock or in the depths of the sea. But my bet is on the first scenario. It never was on Paxton Point."

"You are probably, right, Hilly," Brody said. "I just don't know how to thank you for what you did.

"No need," I said. "Knowing you and Ruby are safe is thanks enough. I just wish that somehow I could bring Gina back."

"You and me both," Brody said. "Oh. The nurse is here, I got to go. I will be home soon and we'll see you then."

"Fine. Don't let them send you home until you feel better and you've got some support set up for Ruby. Has she spoken or signed at all?"

"No, but I think it is because of the sedatives they gave her. I hope when that wears off she'll start communicating again. Meanwhile, I pray."

"Good night and God bless, Brody."

"Same to you, Hilly, our guardian angel." He hung up.

Hoo boy, he's getting a bit maudlin. Seeing me as a guardian angel. I was a friend, a long-time friend. And friends look out for friends. And sometimes, they almost get shot by a madman for their friends.

"Time for bed, Heidi," I said. And we went upstairs.

Chapter 21

A week had gone by since Ralph had been captured. Brody and Ruby were back home. Both of them were suffering from shock and grief.

Brody had no broken bones, but a lot of bruising from the beating Ralph had given him. Ruby didn't have a mark on her. Her scars were deeper and would take more time to deal with. She had started getting therapy at the hospital in Roxton and that would continue with the support of local resources. She didn't appear to have any residual effects from the drugs Ralph had used on her. She was back to signing, but hadn't tried to utter a word. When anyone mentioned her mother, she would walk away and sit in a corner.

Gina's funeral had been held a couple of days ago and both and Brody had found it difficult to attend. Ruby had cried throughout and Brody looked ashen.

A week later, Andrew was still living out at the cottage on the point. Brody had hired him to help out with the rental business on a part-time basis until school ended in two weeks, and then full time till the end of August.

"He's grown up a lot this past couple of weeks," Brody said as we sat outside in the sun. It was a lovely day. Ruby was sitting with Andrew watching him paint a replacement screen door for one of the rental cottages. They were about the same age and had known each other since they were babies, so they got on well.

Brody nodded towards them "It's also good for her to have him around. She needs to know more people of her own age, not be around grownups all the time."

"That's true," I said. "Heck, that's why we used to hang out, to get away from our parents."

Brody smiled. "I remember. I remember too well." A cloud passed over his face and the smile vanished. "Hilly, I miss her more and more each day. I don't know if I will ever have a day when something doesn't set me off wandering through my memories. That's where Andrew is a godsend. He reminds me of things that need doing when instead I am daydreaming. I can't rely on him, forever though so I hope I can back in control of my life."

"It will take time, Brody," I said. "Everyone feels that way when they lose someone they love. It took me a long time not to expect my dad to be sitting on the front porch when I came home. I can still see him sitting there, reading his favorite books, puffing away on his pipe. I wish over and over he had given that pipe up. Maybe he would have lived longer. I could have had more time with him."

"I hear you," Brody said. "Who's that?" He stood up and shaded his eyes.

I looked in the same direction and saw a small red car making its way up the point road. Since Ralph's attack on him, Brody was visibly nervous every time a car pulled onto the point road. I didn't blame him.

"Don't know the car," I said. "Could it be that new therapist that was coming to work with Ruby?"

"No, she's coming tomorrow."

The red car slowed and parked at the side of the cottage. When the door opened, a young woman got out. She waved. "Hi, Hilly.

"It's Louisa, the young librarian, the one who was helping Gina with her research," I told Brody as I went forward to greet her. "Brody, Louisa. Louisa, Brody, Gina's husband."

"Oh, it is so great to meet you, Mr. Paxton," she burbled. "Ms. Paxton talked about you so much. We miss her down at the library. A wonderful person. So sorry for your loss."

Brody fought to keep his tears under control at the mention of Gina's name. He managed a weak "thank you."

"What's up, Louisa?" I asked, stepping in to give Brody a chance to recover.

"Well, I just got in some research material that Ms. Paxton ordered – we couldn't access this material online – it wasn't digitized – so we had to order hard copies and they just came in the mail. I knew this project of hers was part of what, um, what happened. I wasn't sure if I should take this to Lester Spriggs or Mr. Paxton. Since your wife was the customer who ordered and paid for it, Donna told me to deliver it here and let you decide what to do with it." She took a stamped and folded manila envelope out of her tote bag and handed it to Brody.

"Thanks so much, Louisa," I said. "Would you something, coffee?"

"No, no, I'm using work time to do this. Donna thought we should extend the courtesy of a personal delivery instead of calling and asking Mr. Paxton to come down and get it. I have to get back. She's a stickler for accounting for your time and enforcing rules."

I laughed. "That's Donna all right," I said. "She was a hall monitor in school."

"That explains it," Louise said chuckling. "Well, good bye." She climbed back into her little car, turned it around and headed back down the point to the shore road.

"I wonder what Gina ordered," I said.

"Let's go have another cup of coffee and have a look," Brody said. "It was kind of her to bring it here in person."

I poured two cups of coffee and brought them to the kitchen table where Brody had spread out the contents of the envelope. There were three or four articles about the robbery from very old publications dating from the 1930s.

"Hilly," Brody said. "I can't look at this stuff. I never want to hear about this stuff again. You look at it and then put it with the rest of that damn file. I'm going back to sit outside with Ruby and Andrew."

"That's fine, Brody. I understand."

He grabbed his coffee cup and went out, banging the screen door behind him. I settled down to read the articles. Two of them were similar to everything else I had read – one about the robbery itself – and the other about Dan's capture and subsequent death from the gunshot wounds he received in the shootout.

The third, however, was different. First of all, it wasn't a newspaper article at all and it dated from about a year after Dan had died. Secondly, it was from a church magazine. It contained an interview with Dan's sister who had been a church member. It was interesting reading. She talked about her wicked brother who had lied, stolen and killed, getting his just desserts, dying from gunshot wounds. And, the article proved the press reports that Dan never uttered a word while he was in the hospital were false. He had been under constant police guard, it was true, but his sister claimed she and her pastor had been allowed to sit with him in his final hours. She had been praying when he suddenly reached out and grabbed her hand.

"Then he spoke and I knew that God had touched his heart. He had repented and found the Lord's forgiveness. I sat there praying and holding his hand, crying, while he kept repeating the words, the Lamb of God the Lamb of God that taketh away the sins, the sins, oh the Lamb of God, remember the Lamb of God."

Then she said he collapsed and died in her arms. She went on to say that her pastor told her that he had been referring to the text "the Lamb of God that taketh away the sins of the world John 1:29. He said the fact that Dan repeated those words meant that he had finally accepted Jesus in his heart and repented. "It was a miracle," the sister told the interviewer.

"Wow," I said. "What an exit line." There was a picture with the article showing Dan and another unidentified man. The sister said she took the photo when the two men visited her for her birthday about three days before the bank robbery. The second man was not named, but there was something about the way he put his hand on his hip, a mannerism I'd seen before.

I went out to the front porch.

"Anything interesting." Brody asked.

"Could be," I said and gave him the short version of the church magazine article.

"He repented and raved on spouting Bible verses. He was probably delirious and had no idea what he was saying," Brody commented. "From what Chrissie said in her journal, Dan did not seem like the religious type."

"Well, be that as it may, people often panic and find religion when they know they are going to die," I said. "It's been documented."

Brody snorted. "Some maybe, but him, I doubt it. The way he killed all his accomplices – and leaving Elmont's body in the rowboat for Chrissie and Myron to find – that's just sick."

"I know, I know. But Brody don't you have an old photo album around here somewhere? I remember Gina once showing me it. The photos were from the early part of the 20th century. I think there was one of Elmont."

"Sure," Brody said. "Don't know what you think you'll get from it." He sounded grumpy

"Pill time? I asked, gently. The doctor had prescribed an analgesic to help with the pain of the deep bruising from the beating he got from Ralph. I knew he was slowly feeling better but still had a lot of healing to do. Luckily, he had no broken bones.

Brody looked at me. "Yes."

"Okay." I lead the way back into the kitchen.

"Sorry, was I grumpy?" he asked.

"You are always grumpy when you are in pain, always have been."

"You know me too well," he said, taking a prescription bottle out of the kitchen cabinet and depositing a capsule in the palm of his hand. He swigged the pill down with the remains of his coffee. Then put the bottle back in the cupboard.

"I think the album is in the storage closet at the end of the hall." He led the way down the hall to a closed door which opened into what was once a small bedroom. Its mission in life changed when Brody's father had decided he needed more room for his collection of model sailboats. Now it housed necessary extra items plus family heirlooms and piles of junk. Gina always vowed she was going to clear it all out, but never seemed to find the time.

Brody pulled a couple of old photo albums off the shelf. "Think what you are looking for may be in one of these," he said.

"Thanks. Go back and relax," I said. "I'll look through them."

"Fine. I am really enjoying that sun today. You need to get out into it, Hilly. All this staying inside isn't good for you,"

"I know, Brody. I'll be out shortly. I just want to confirm something."

"Good luck." He left and I heard the screen door slam shut a minute later.

I toted the heavy albums to the kitchen table. They weren't as dusty as I thought they would be which meant someone had been looking at them recently. Gina probably. I opened the first one and saw women in long skirts, Edwardian men's outfits and some World War One uniforms. I didn't look all the way through that album because. I figured it covered an era that was too early for what I wanted. I shut it and reached for the next one. But that one started out with World War two uniforms, and then went on to feature women in poodle skirts. Too late a period, so I shut that one and went to the very back of the first album I had picked up.

Yes, 1930s style dresses and blurry photos of the point. I flipped towards the front of the book and, a few pages in, there was the photo I was looking for. It showed a young man standing beside a cemetery crypt with two other young men. They were all smoking and one held a bottle of some kind of alcohol in one hand. In the background you could see two young women. Elmont stood in the odd but familiar pose with one hand on his hip. Underneath the photo was written, in neat writing, "Cousin Elmont, 1931, with friends."

There was no doubt in my mind; it was definitely the same young man in the photo with Dan that had been published in the church magazine. Somewhere along the line, after he left Texas, Elmont had hooked up with Dan and become a bank robber. I was pleased with myself for making the connection. But I didn't feel like celebrating.

I get a tickle in my brain that I can't scratch when things are coming together. I knew that somehow everything I had learned connected to something, but what?

"Old photos, I love old photos." Andrew suddenly appeared and hung over my shoulder pointing. "Who's Elmont? What kind of a name is that?"

"It's old-fashioned," I replied. "Who knows where it comes from? Probably someone's family name."

"Hey, cool," Andrew said. "They are standing in front of this really neat old crypt we saw when our history class toured the cemetery a few weeks back. Did I tell you about it?"

"No, you didn't. What's so cool about the crypt?"

"The old caretaker, he was a really odd dude and I could tell he didn't like teenagers. He made a big point of telling us that the only reason that crypt was locked behind a high iron fence was because young people used to go in there, drink and 'party" as he put it. I think he meant they had sex there."

"Oh really, too much information, Andrew."

He chuckled. "Does that word bother you, Hilly? Sex?"

"No, but it will bother your mother if she hears you bandying it about like that."

"Bandying?"

"Never mind. So what crypt is this, did they tell you?"

"Of course, it was one of the highlights of our history tour. It's the Josiah Lamb family crypt."

I stared at him. "Are you sure this is the same crypt?" I asked. I peered at the photo

"Here try this," Andrew said, handing me a magnifying glass.

"Where did you get that?"

"Shh, don't tell Uncle Brody. He sometimes uses it to read the newspaper – I think he needs glasses, but he's too proud to get them."

That sounded like Brody. Andrew and I bent over the photo again, this time with the magnifying glass, "Oh that's it, all right," Andrew said.

"How do you know? I think all crypts look alike –lots of stonework, inscriptions, creepy statues."

"No creepy status on this one," he said. "All it has this great big lamb on the top – see?" He pointed to the photo again.

I saw. On top of the crypt, there was a blurry outline of a stone lamb.

Andrew continued. "I asked the teacher why, I mean as you said, most crypts we saw that day had gargoyles and stuff like that on them, even angels. But a sheep?"

"What did she say?"

"She quoted a Latin phrase to me. Said it meant the Lamb of God which is Jesus and something about being absolved of your sins. Old Josiah must have had a lot of sins to go so far as to put that ugly lamb statue on his crypt."

I gasped. "Andrew. You are a genius."

"Why?"

"You just solved it," I said jumping to my feet and giving him a hug.

He stepped back and looked at me perplexed. "Solved what?" he asked.

"Brody," I shouted heading for the door onto the porch. "We just figured it out."

Chapter 22

We made an odd procession the seven of us: the cemetery caretaker, Lester, Harry, Brody, Andrew – of course – and Sid toting a folding ladder. Initially Andrew wasn't supposed to be along on this expedition but, as he pointed out, that if the Josiah Lamb crypt was the solution to the mystery of the missing gold bars, he was the one who had come up with the major clue.

As we neared the crypt, I noticed the tall iron fence around it. It was higher than most I'd seen around a crypt. They really must have had a big problem with young people partying there. I could see why. The crypt itself was big and so was the plot it stood on. There was plenty of room to party. In addition, the crypt was set in a corner of the cemetery and surrounded by tall trees on three sides, affording privacy. The building itself had impressive It had a stone arched entry, Grecian-style columns and was built of gray marble. Standing on top of the steep roof was a large statue of a lamb. There was no mistaking which family owned that crypt. Josiah Lamb had done well by himself and his descendants. I knew the former family mansion was sitting empty and probably needed some care but the last heir had died the previous year. However, this crypt would last a few hundred years more.

"When were the fence and the gates installed," I asked "1935," the caretaker replied. "Too many complaints about young fellows partying down here," he said, glaring at Andrew." The caretaker selected a key from a big ring full of them and unlocked the gate's padlock.

"You won't do any damage or commit any acts of desecration will you," he asked.

"We're the police, Arnold," Lester said, giving him a reassuring pat on the shoulder. "We don't desecrate though we do arrest and incarcerate."

"Oh," Arnold said, obviously puzzled by the attempt at a joke. He led the way to the crypt's front door. He unlocked that and ushered us inside. It was dark and gloomy in there, despite the light from our flashlights.

Coffins in various states of decay sat on the two shelves that lined the walls to the right and left. Straight ahead of us were raised a crucifix and a bench, presumably for any family members visiting who wanted to pray. Above the bench was another statue of the lamb and underneath it, the following text.

"Agnus dei qui tollis peccata mundi, miserere nobis."

"My guess is Latin," Lester said.

"The lamb of god who taketh away the sins of the world, have mercy on us," I said. "Thank god father made me learn my classics."

"And you think this means the gold is stashed here?" Lester asked.

"It all fits," Andrew blurted. "The quotes Dan said when he was dying, the clues leading to the lamb – but not Lamb's Bay nor the old rock formation. Elmont knew this place. So it's a no brainer."

We all stared at Andrew

"Planning on taking an apprentice, Hilly?" Lester asked.

"Maybe," I replied. "So can we look? I mean, maybe they hid the gold behind or in one of these coffins. Or could it be up in the roof supports?"

The caretaker looked horrified. "You can't search this place without permission from the authorities and you certainly can't open coffins," he said.

"I am the authorities," Lester said. "And as for the family, as far as anyone knows the last member of the Josiah Lamb family passed away last year. I don't think anyone is about to materialize and sue us for conducting a search."

Arnold looked stricken. "Well, I wouldn't want to see any . . ."

"I know," Lester said. "No desecration. Look, why don't you and Brody wait outside. There not that much room in here. We can look around and let you know what we find."

"Please be careful," he said as Brody led him back into the sunlight.

"Okay," Lester said. "Fan out. Use your flashlights and Sid; get that ladder thing unfolded so we can check the top shelves."

We gave the place a careful once-over, but there were no immediate signs of any bag or box that could contain the gold bars.

"Unfortunately, that means if it is here, that it is probably in one of these coffins," Lester said. "Andrew, I want you to go out there and keep the caretaker talking. I don't want him to see us checking out the coffin contents. He'll have a fit."

"But I want to see," Andrew said.

"Another day," Lester said. "If you do as I say, I'll get the coroner to let you visit the morgue one day. How's that?"

"Cool," Andrew said and went outside. I could hear him cross-examining the caretaker about the crypt and the cemetery.

"Debbie is going have a fit if he grows up to be a homicide detective," I said.

"Hey, there's worse jobs," Lester said. "Anything up there, Harry?"

Harry was up on the mini ladder and poking around a coffin in the far corner of the top shelf. "Hey," he said. "This coffin has been disturbed."

"How can you tell?" Lester asked.

"All the others are lying straight, but this one is crooked," Harry said. "But I need help to move it out so I can look behind."

Sid used the shelves to climb to the top so he could help Harry and together they moved the coffin ahead a few inches.

"Nothing," Harry said, "but wait. This lid isn't sitting right."

"What?" Lester asked.

"Yeah," Harry said. "Looks like it has been opened. Okay if we open it?"

Lester and I checked out the door. The caretaker was holding forth on the history of the cemetery to Brody and Andrew.

"Go for it," Lester said.

Together Sid and Harry pushed the lid sideways, just enough to see inside. I heard a low chuckle and swung my flashlight up just in time to see Harry grinning from ear to ear. Sid was smiling too.

"So?" Lester asked.

Harry and Sid climbed down. "I think you and Hilly need to see this for yourselves," Harry said.

I took the ladder and Lester used the shelves to climb up. As we shone our flashlights into the coffin, instead of seeing a skeleton all nicely laid out, we saw a pile of bones at one end of the coffin and at the other – the missing gold bars.

"Well I'll be damned," Lester said. "Hilly, go talk to the caretaker and send Brody in – he needs to see what all the fuss has been about and what caused his wife's death."

I went out and motioned Brody to step inside. The caretaker was now well into his recitation of cemetery development and had reached the 1960s. He was lamenting the fact that cremation had become more popular. "Just simple urns in the columbarium," he moaned. "No elegant headstones or crypts any more. So awful."

I nodded sagely. "Yes, very awful." Now no one would be able to hide stolen loot in fancy stone crypts. Really awful.

Chapter 23

The news that the treasure had been recovered hit the media. There had been a lot of publicity about the case following Ralph and Carl's arrests for the murders of Janet and Gina. And the fact that they had been looking for the gold in the wrong place – as had everybody since the 1930s – was big news.

The poor caretaker at the cemetery was beseiged by reporters wanting to take photos of the crypt. Lester provided police protection to ensure there was no desecration.

The gold was returned to the banking chain that had bought out the original bank it was stolen from. Lester made sure they honored the original reward offered in 1934. $500 – but in today's dollars and that Brody got the credit for figuring out where the gold had been hidden. It was a nice hunk of cash and Brody planned to stash it away in an account to use for Ruby and anything she might need.

Debbie was having fits because Andrew had announced his intention of studying harder and improving his marks – she was in agreement with that goal – but was not happy that he was planning to do this so he could go to police school.

"Leave him be, Debbie," I said. "There's a couple of years before he makes that decision and he might change it. In the meantime, anything that gets him interested in school is a good thing." She finally agreed but added she hoped he would change his mind.

I sat on the back porch one evening with Brody. A couple of days before, we had all gathered to say our final good-bye to Gina. Brody had opted to cast her ashes into the sea off the point. He said she always loved it there and he couldn't bear the thought of confining her spirit to the grave. We were all looking out for Brody as he transitioned through this sad time.

I'd asked him to come over for supper. Debbie had offered to have Ruby for the night so Brody and I could talk. We'd barbequed. The weather had turned warm and humid. It made you feel lazy. Heidi, minus stitches but still wearing her cone, was snoozing in the shade.

"So there never was a treasure in Paxton Point," Brody said. "How could so many people be so wrong for so many years? All they had to do is what Gina did. Research."

"Research is very important," I said. "It pays my bills."

Brody smiled. "Thanks, Hilly."

"For what?"

"For being there, for decoding all that material she accumulated, for being smarter than all of us and figuring it out."

"Andrew deserves part of that honour," I said. "He still going to live with you for the summer?"

"Yeah, Debbie has enough on her hands with the other four. And Ruby and I like the company. So Hilly . . ."

"So, what?"

"The dog?"

"Oh, Heidi, well, I haven't heard from Zach and I don't want to."

"But isn't he going to ask for her back?"

"I'll deal with that when it happens. Right now, I'm enjoying her company."

Brody's cell dinged. He looked at it. "Damn. One of the cottagers says the toilet is overflowing and he doesn't know what to do. City folk. Going to have to call it a night, Hilly. Thanks again for dinner."

"You are very welcome," I said.

"Don't bother to walk me out. I know the way. You look very comfortable there with your wine and your, well, the dog."

"Bye." I said.

He disappeared inside and, a few minutes later I heard his car start and pull away from the house.

The sky was reddening in the west. Brilliant shades of blue, green and yellow streaked across the sky, turning the sunset into a brilliant piece of modern art, fit for any museum in the country. A ray shot down and washed over Heidi's golden fur, making it a richer shade. She yawned and rolled over so I could scratch her belly.

"Red sky at night, sailor's delight," I told her. "Tomorrow should be a great day."

We sat there watching the light show until it faded and stars began to dot the darkening sky. Never again would treasure hunters disturb the peace of Paxton Point. Things were back to normal in Lamb's Bay.

About the Author

A.J. Fotheringham

A. J. Fotheringham is a Montreal-based writer and editor, who
has published children's, fiction, short stories,
poetry and non-fiction.
A career communications professional, she is a graduate of
McGill University and Seton Hill University in Pittsburgh.

To learn more about me, visit my website
and check out my blog "Let's Talk Writing" at:

www.ajfotheringham.com

Manufactured by Amazon.ca
Bolton, ON

17810877R00116